I0629848

Forbidden Runes

The Caster Chronicles, Volume 1

Brandi A. Mendenhall

Published by Brandi A. Mendenhall, 2022.

This is a work of fiction. Similarities to real people, places, or events are entirely coincidental.

FORBIDDEN RUNES

First edition. August 22, 2022.

In loving memory of my little 'big' brother: Edmund A. Mendenhall. I did it little bro...I took the leap, finished the novel, and have now published.

Also in loving memory of my writing buddy and forever furbaby: Max.

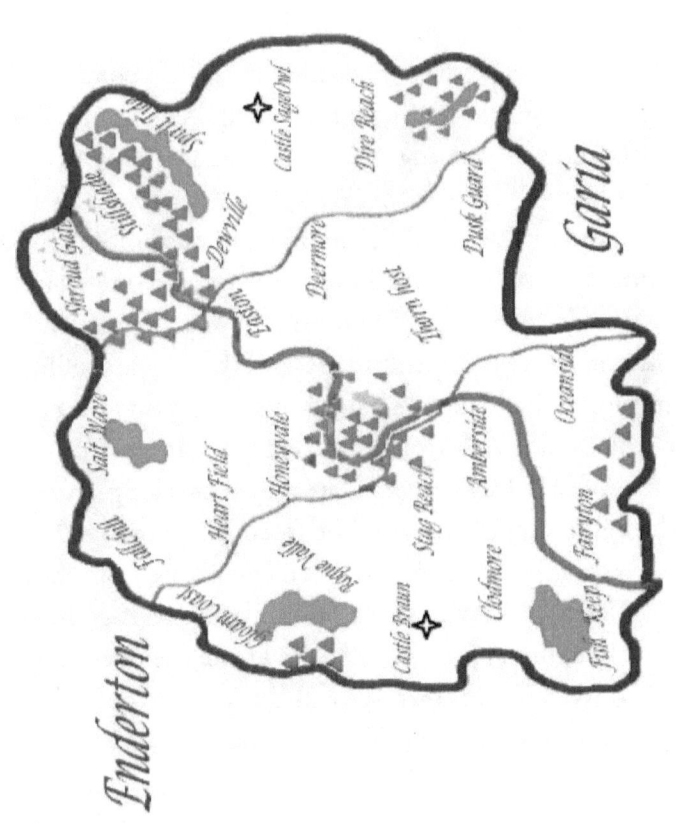

Prologue

Anna – 5 years old

"Aylex, they are outside in the forecourt..." Lily breathed harshly as she rushed into their daughter's room. The sage green skirts she was wearing swished alarmingly around her legs. "You must hurry!"

"Almost there..." Aylex huffed. He was holding his daughter in a bear hug, tight against his purple vest. No one would have a clue he was doing anything, unless they were a Rune Caster, and even then, it was very difficult to see the ethereal glow of light. The glow enveloped his daughter's head, his eyes flashed a bright shade of purple, and then he fought to keep his tears at bay.

"Aylex..." Lily snapped. She pulled two long silver daggers from the belt around her waist. She faced the door, hands up, prepared. Each dagger had a sheen of green emanating from the blades.

"It's done." Aylex turned to his wife and together they hugged their daughter. Her eyes still closed from the powerful rune casting. "We love you, baby girl. We will always love you."

"Your Highnesses!" Teamalah grasped the little girl and pulled her from their grip. "You must come with me. I can save you all!"

"No, Teamalah..." Aylex sighed softly and pulled his sword. His weapon emanated purple rune symbols as he held it. "Someone has to survive for our kingdom. Lily and I are the last defense. Take her, hide her, raise her as your own, and when the time is right, help her take back our kingdom! Now go!!!!" he shouted just as the door crashed open.

Teamalah clutched a still sleeping five-year-old to her chest, tears streaming down her face as she turned from the imminent massacre. She locked the memory of the king and queen defending their kingdom in her brain. She would share this one day with their daughter. Her eyes dropped to the child in her arms as she ran. She was her daughter now. The thought of anyone harming a child was beyond incomprehensible to her. It would take the Goddess herself to rip this child from her. She would protect her with every fiber of her being.

She half wished she was a Rune Caster. She could protect her even more. Even so, her feet were still quick for being thirty. She darted quickly into the kings' chamber and shut the door, throwing the bar in place as she turned to find the hidden recess that she had accidentally found one day. It had been somewhere near the desk in his study. She rushed to the desk and began moving books and statues with one hand.

The book of fantasy tales for children clicked as she moved it and she let out a relieved sigh. The bookcase slowly moved into the wall. She sat her charge on the dusty and dirty stairs, using both arms to shove the bookcase back into place. She could surely spare a moment to breath. In this dark and dirty passage behind the walls of the castle, she could take a moment to grieve the loss of her king and queen. She stood there, holding the bookcase closed, knowing that she needed to get moving.

"Mama..." the girl said groggily, rubbing at her eyes. "Mama..."

"I'm here child..." Teamalah responded, turning and scooping her back into her arms.

"Why is it dark?" she whimpered, tears starting in her little eyes.

"I need you to use your power my child...just a little...like a firefly, can you do that?" Teamalah silently thanked the Goddess as the little girl in her arms disappeared completely in the darkness, turning blacker than black, then a small orb of light appeared in the air. "That's it my precious. Hold that...just for a little bit and keep quiet."

"But mama..." she cried. "I don't like the dark." Teamalah had started running as fast as she dared with the dim light showing the way.

"I know baby..." she panted. "Just a little longer..." she begged.

It seemed like forever as they plunged through the cobwebs of the dark passage. The sounds of fighting grew louder and then disappeared. The clashing of weapons, screaming of men and women, and loud crashing sounds grew as she stopped to catch her breath at the end of the hidden passageway. She could see a faint outline around the hidden door. She sent another quick prayer to the Goddess as she felt around for the latch. The click and groan as the stones grated against each other sent shivers down her spine. Surely the cacophony of the fighting was loud enough no one would hear it, right? She pushed, crouching as low as she could while holding the child. Poking her head out, she let out a soft whoop of triumph. All the fighting was at the front of the castle. None of the dissenters had made it this far into the back garden.

She looked across the moonlit garden, hoping that the horse she had hidden was still there. She gulped in three deep breaths, pushed the hidden entrance closed, flinched once more at the sound of the grating stones, then tucked the child against her chest a little tighter and ran through the gardens. She hopped over gardenia bushes, rushed through a field of lilies, and darted past jasmine vines, looking for the maze where she had stashed a horse only hours earlier. Where was the damned beast! She turned the corner from a statue of the king and queen, around a wall of roses and sighed with relief as the horse nickered quietly. The beast was busy tearing off rose heads and chewing in delight. Teamalah shoved the child into the saddle and then quickly climbed up behind her.

"Alright Ala...uh Anna, you can let go of your light."

"Where are we mama?" she asked with a terrified sob as Teamalah whipped the horse into a gallop towards the northern forests.

"We were visiting some friends." Teamalah choked on her tears as she looked behind her. She could see large fires engulfing the stables. Thank the Goddess she had enough forethought to stash a horse in the garden. "We were just visiting some dear friends. Now we are heading off to visit the elves and then if you are a good girl, we are going to visit the dwarves. You think you can handle that?"

"I promise I will be very good!" Anna squealed with delight, the tears instantly drying on her cheek as she clapped her hands. "I can't wait to meet them."

"And meet them you shall my princess..." Teamalah promised as she whipped the horse to go faster.

• • • •

ANNA – 10 YEARS OLD

Anna stood precariously on the edge of the river bank, reaching as far as she could, the herb she wanted just barely out of her reach. She moved just a smidge closer, feeling the water as it began to soak into her leather boots. She stretched once more. Her fingers just barely grazed the stalk of the herb. She heard a commotion behind her, turned her head, and lost her footing on the edge. Tumbling head first into the water, Anna splashed and spluttered, shoving back to her feet, now completely soaked. The sound of male laughter assaulted her ears and she flipped her wet brown hair out of her face. She put her hands on her hips and glared at the two boys. One boy was slightly taller than the other. The taller of the two had black hair, brown eyes, and was wearing glaring white breeches and a tunic. His boots were the cleanest pair of boots she had ever seen. She turned her gaze to the shorter of the two and noticed he had dark brown hair, blue eyes, and dimples as he smiled. This boy was wearing clean boots, a pair of black breeches and a pumpkin-colored tunic. Both looked as if they had just bathed that morning.

"Why are you clodpolls laughing?" she demanded as she grabbed the elusive herb she had been after. She opened the flap on her bag at her hip and shoved it inside, cringing at how full of water the bag was. She tried to adjust her plain brown skirt and tunic to resemble something better than the drowned rat she now appeared to be.

"You looked just like one of those fish that jump around in the water..." the shorter one guffawed, holding his orange clad sides as he continued to laugh.

"It *was* fairly comical..." the taller one said with a wink. He snickered, but otherwise cut off his laughter, clearing his throat, standing up straight, and tugging on the hem of his tunic. "Why would you even be reaching into the river in the first place?"

Anna stormed past the two boys, aiming a well-placed foot to stomp on the taller one's gleaming leather boot, satisfied to see she had left a trail of mud. He yelped, grabbing his foot and hopping around. She smiled and began laughing as the shorter of the two began howling with mirth so hard he fell to the ground, rolling around, snuffling and snorting.

"Well, if I looked like a jumping fish, you sir, look like a pig rolling in a sty." She turned her angry gaze to the tall one who was now limping around in circles, his head tossed back, his breaths puffing from his chest. "And you sir, you looked like a monkey hopping around like that."

"Well..." the taller one groaned as he finally stood straight without flinching. "I must say that we are a sight...all of us animals out here..."

"Yeah! Hey, we could do that, Ben. Let's play menagerie."

"Naw...there is only two of us. It wouldn't be much fun to play menagerie with only two of us." The taller one, Ben, turned to look at her. "I'm Ben and this is Mikal. We were trying to decide what we were going to do today. Would you like to join us for a game?"

"I'm Anna..." she dipped her head at them but then sniffed and tilted her head back slightly. "I can't. I have to help mama and papa today."

"Are you helping by jumping in the river like a fish?" Mikal snickered.

"Yes...I mean...no!" Anna snapped. "Mama and papa are very important people. They are the herbalists to the King and Queen. We are only this far out in Border Town to collect some of the rarer herbs that we can't find closer to the castle. I don't have time for childish games."

"Childish..." Ben tilted his head and crossed his arms over his chest. "I am twelve thank you! I don't play childish games."

"Yeah...and I'm ten!" Mikal crowed, trying to mimic his brother's indignant stance.

"So?" Anna flipped her still wet hair over her shoulder and turned to follow the river. "I'm ten myself, but I am way more grown up than you two!"

"We shall see about that..." Ben snarked as she disappeared around the bend. "Come on Mikal. I'm sure mother and father will be more than happy to invite some people over when we get back."

"Oh, guests...I'm down for that. It means all the good foods." He picked up a stick and began whacking the trees as they walked. "Just not her...she is way too snooty! She shouldn't get any of those meat pies."

• • • •

ANNA TUGGED ON HER brown lock of hair. Her parents had dragged her to the castle as soon as they got back from border town. Her mother had shoved two small parcels into her hands and insisted that she give the gifts to the princes. She was now standing in this stuffy boring parlor room waiting for the princes to be brought in. The room was large, holding an ornate wooden hand carved mahogany desk, a large wing back upholstered chair with gold braid, and two smaller chairs padded with velvet and trimmed in gold braid in front of the desk. There were three bookshelves hand carved from mahogany with vines and leaves that lined the wall behind the desk, all full to bursting with statutes, rocks, books, sheafs of parchments, and other such things. The books were all leather bound and gold leaf stamped. The desktop was polished and gleaming in the candlelight in the gold sconces on the wall. She tried not to gag at how lavish this room was. She turned her gaze behind her and noticed there were two closed doors to the right. She wondered what was in there that they didn't want them to see. She was currently seated on the royal blue velvet chaise with her mother, the King and Queen were seated across from them in the upholstered wing back chairs.

Jasper, her father, was walking around the room, admiring the books on the shelves and the artwork in gilt frames. There was a hand carved mahogany table between the two sofas and it was currently holding cups that were trimmed in gold and a pot of tea. Anna wrapped the lock of hair she was tugging around her finger and yanked again when the door opened. She shot off the couch and turned just as those two clodpolls from the river walked in. They were both dressed in dark blue formal looking attire with golden buttons and golden braid decoration. Both were wearing white hose and polished black heels. They ambled in proudly, dipping soft bows to the guests in the room, snarky smiles on their faces. Anna giggled, snorted, and then grasped her sides laughing.

"You two look like girls in those hose!" she teased.

"We do not!" Mikal whined, his head dipping, his cheeks flaming, his hands twisting the gold buttons on his coat.

Ben did not react, only stood there, waiting for her laughter to die down. It was at that moment he was struck with how lovely a girl she was. The red of her cheeks highlighted those bright doe eyes, her pink lips curving up in a smile. Her long brown hair curled slightly, hanging loose around her face. She was wearing a pale pink dress that hugged her body but flared out around her long stick like legs. He watched as she tugged on a curl, making the pink bow in her hair bounce, and inhaled deeply. Her hands dropped to her dress skirt, pulling out two small parcels. She thrust them into their hands, her cheeks turning redder. He watched as she dipped a perfect curtsy and then stood.

"My apologies, Your Highnesses..." She tilted her head, looking up at him. "I brought gifts in honor of being invited to the castle."

"We thank you." Ben tucked the parcel into his pocket and motioned to the door. "Would you like to join us? We were just getting ready to change out of these girly clothes and into something we could go riding in." He gave her a coy smile.

"I'd love to go riding..." Anna replied, turning to look at her parents. They both smiled at her warmly and she turned around, beaming. "I'll meet you in the stable!"

• • • •

ANNA – 18 YEARS OLD

Ben approached her, the look of need burning in his eyes. He didn't dare touch her, not yet. She had to be willing. Her body backed up two baby steps for every single step he took. He wasn't backing down. He wanted her. He had wanted her for a very long time and he showed her in every way he could. He projected that need into his face, his movements, his body, and even his mind as he pressed her further back. It wasn't until she ran into the trunk of the tree that she stopped backing up. Her brown eyes gazed into his. She swallowed and licked those perfectly shaped pink lips. His eyes watched that tongue as it swept her full bottom lip.

Oh, how he wanted to taste those lips. He bet she tasted like honey and spice and everything nice. He held his meager distance, waiting. Either she would break and be his, or she would run. There was no other option when he used his power. He inhaled deeply, catching all the scents carried on the gentle evening air, but more importantly, catching her scent. She smelled of lavender and lilacs. His eyes flashed with white light; his face slightly brighter than normal. His mind was wrapped up with images of how he would take her and how the heavens would sing when he did. He leaned forward slightly, taking a few more inches from her, his lips hovering a hairs breadth away. He heard her moan softly, deep in her throat, almost like a purr. His power was working. How long before she broke?

"We can't..." she whispered. The sounds of the river burbled quietly to their left. The night forest animals were slowly increasing adding to the noise.

"We can..." he rasped. The need for her was setting his body on fire. He needed the release of his power. He needed her. He wasn't sure how long he could wait. He would not be like the others who flamed out from their power.

"Ben..." she licked her lips again, tilting her head up to him. "It is...impossible..."

"No..." he chuckled lightly, grazing her oh so soft lips with his. They breathed the same air. He could feel her heart beat against his. "Not impossible. Just say the words my lovely and I am yours."

"Ben..." she sighed. Then, as if she woke from a dream, she pressed her head back, her body going rigid, her hands fell from almost touching his chest. Her eyes seemed to flash with blackness. "NO." She cleared her throat. "NO!" she said with a firmer voice.

Ben reeled, almost as if she had physically slapped him. He stumbled two steps back. The passion and need still simmering under his skin and in his veins, but he couldn't see the images of their bodies entwined any more. His skin stopped glowing. It was as if she had channeled some unforeseen force to push him and his power away. Her doe-colored eyes were hard as flint. Her chin was thrust up in defiance. Her body was taut with controlled anger. He took another shaky step away, trying to reconcile what was in his mind with what he was seeing. She should have succumbed to his rune casting. She should have begged him to take her. All the other girls he had used his casting on had succumbed within seconds.

She cast aside his mental assault as if he wasn't casting. Her cheeks were red and flushed so tantalizingly. Her lips seemed a little fuller than a moment ago, almost as if he had actually kissed her. Her shoulder length brown hair was flying wildly around her head like he had just thrust his hands into it. Her chest heaved up and down. Yet she still resisted his assault. This was completely unheard of. Never had a female been able to stand up to his power. He was the most powerful white rune caster in all the lands. How could this girl, the one he had known all his life, how could she possibly be able to resist him?

"Enough Ben. I'll not have you ruin our friendship over your silly manly need. There are tavern wenches in the village who would be willing to help you with that."

"How can you...?" he stammered.

"I've been around you my whole life, Ben." She crossed her arms over her chest and stomped her foot like an angry school girl. "You don't think that at some point I have mustered up enough resistance against that cursed white rune power you possess?"

"But..."

"NO!" She mentally pressed on the orb of her own power, the anger rolling off her in waves, her eyes flashing black once more. She took a step forward and inwardly cheered herself when he took a step back. "Damn you royalty, always thinking any commoner would take a tumble with you just to have the pleasure. I may be a commoner Prince Ben, but I will not sully our relationship that way. Go cool off in the stream or take a wench from the tavern. I'll not be speaking with you again until your power has cooled." She flung her hand violently out in the direction of the river. "GO!"

Ben took off quickly towards the river, his feet not slowing even as he hit the river bank. He jumped and dived into the cold waters.

The shock of the cold water cooled his passion and reset his brain. How in Gaia had Anna done that? Not only did she force him to stop casting his power at her, but she had somehow forced a mental cast of her own for him to jump in the river. Shivering, he climbed up onto the river bank and sat gasping for air, his passion now firmly under wraps. The late fall evening had been comfortable but the slight breeze after his cold dip was making him a frozen icicle. He swiped the hair from his eyes and let out a huff.

Goddess bless that woman for keeping him from making a fool of himself. He could see it now that he was clearheaded. He could also see that he was falling for her. He wouldn't call it love. He couldn't love her. He was a prince and she was a peasant, but he couldn't imagine what life would be like without her. He forced himself up off the river bank and towards his horse. He had to find out if there was a rune power capable of equaling or besting his. He had never heard of it. His parents surely would have told him, right? Swiping angrily at the hair covering his forehead as he rode into the courtyard, he vaulted off his horse, tossed his reins to a stable boy, and rushed inside only to halt quickly. The sounds of his parents conferring behind their chamber door was never a good sign...not in those tones.

"Ben has an unnatural affinity for that girl!" his father growled.

"Now John...you know how teenagers are. They grow fond of each other. It won't last..."

"Minerva...be realistic dear." Ben could see in his mind's eye how his father would pat his wife on her shoulder and give her one of his looks. "Ben is the most powerful white rune caster in the land. With his ardor telepathy, no girl will tell him no. If he sets his mind to being with that peasant girl, Anna..."

"Leave his powers out of it. We raised him right John." Ben could just imagine his mother's annoyed glance at the mention of his power. "He won't take his power to the dark side like the Corrupt King. We won't lose him that way. Besides, it is just a crush. She is eighteen. I am surprised her parents haven't wed her yet. She'll be betrothed to some farmer from the neighboring village soon enough."

"Minerva...I can't leave anything to chance."

"What do you plan to do? Lock her up in the dungeon until Ben forgets about her?"

"If I must..."

Chapter One

Anna wrapped her cloak tighter around her waist and stared at the hand drawn picture on the tree. The parchment was faded and old. She was surprised it was still there it was so withered. The tree had also seen better days. The once proud oak tree seemed to be ready to fall. The leaves were brown even at the height of summer. The bark was peeling, sap running down the length of the trunk. The limbs all looked as if at any moment they would snap and fall to the ground. The girl in that picture had been missing, presumably for twenty years. If she hadn't been found by now, she probably never would be. She looked at the image one more time. That girl looked vaguely familiar. The drawing was pretty crude, almost as if a child had drawn it.

Shuddering, she tugged the hood of her cloak deeper around her face. The village market of Stagreach was pretty crowded this early in the morning. As if to remind herself of her purpose, her stomach growled angrily. Clutching a single coin, the last she had, she walked among the food stalls looking for something she could stomach as well as afford. It had been a while since she had been this far into Enderton, but she couldn't remember it being so downtrodden. The market stalls were all arranged down the middle of the village. The stalls themselves were just wooden tables that had been scrounged up from left over wood piles. The tents were made from patched fabrics held up by saggy poles of wood. The back of the stalls stood against the wooden walls of the businesses they were selling from. Those walls all needed fresh coats of paint, new thatched roofs, and new curtains on the windows. Even the stall sellers needed new clothing. It looked as if they were wearing whatever rags they could find with the fewest holes in them.

Anna finally found an old man, near the end of the market. He was selling some flaccid looking root vegetables. She motioned towards the carrots and held up her single coin. The old man smiled softly and held two very large, but still soft carrots. She nodded, putting the coin in his hand and scooping the carrots up. She was just reaching back into her cloak to put the carrots away when he caught her wrist. Her eyes instantly darted up to his. The man had his head tilted, his eyes squinted turning slightly purple, his mouth was slack. He was a rune caster, she recognized that unseeing look anywhere. Anna waited patiently as the purple light slowly dimmed from his eyes. When he returned to his senses, his mouth pressed into a firm hard line, his grip tightened on her wrist.

"My recommendation is that you move out of Stagreach as fast as you can miss."

"I'm merely passing through." She turned her head to the side as she nibbled on one of the carrots. They were pretty close to expiration, but it was all she could afford. She schooled her face to not sour at the taste of them. "What did you see?"

"Nothing good. People like you and I..." he darted his gaze around as he dropped his voice. "We are best served on the other side of the border. You should make your way back there unless you want to meet your untimely end at the hand of the Corrupt King."

"I have business here." She reached over and patted him softly on the shoulder. "But rest assured my feet will make haste as soon as it is done."

"I'm afraid that won't be fast enough miss..." the man's eyes darted to a guard behind her. He cleared his throat and ducked his head. "If those carrots be to your liking miss..."

"They are delicious." She took a large hunk out of one, feeling her stomach heave, and then turned away from him in the opposite direction of his gaze. It wouldn't do to attract the guard's attention, not when she was so close to her goal.

Anna ambled along the dirt path, stopping here and there at various stalls as she made her way out of the town center. She had heard plenty of rumors from the Garian's. The once peaceful co-existence between the two kingdoms had crumbled in the last twenty years. Anna blamed the new King of Enderton for it, the Corrupt King as he was called. The man hated all rune casters. Immediately after taking the throne, he had banished all rune casters from his kingdom. After a few years of forcing rune casters out, he finally turned to execution. If you were caught in Enderton using the craft, you would be hauled off to the royal dungeon to await sentencing by the King. She had heard plenty about the different types of punishment the Corrupt King came up with, yet she still couldn't find out the reason for his hatred of rune casters.

Anna tugged the hood of her cloak tighter about her as she passed three of the King's guards. She was skimming a little too close to the castle this time for her comfort, but it had to be done. She was here to rescue a child with blue rune craft and she wouldn't fail to save him. For years now she had been sneaking across the border from Garia, testing children and adults alike who were suspected to have rune powers. Once confirmed, she would help them cross the border into Garia, set them up with well-trained casters in their talent, and assist them with making a new life. It was a dangerous path for her to walk, but someone had to look out for their people.

Anna reached the end of the market while still deep in thought. She almost missed the small alley between the businesses and run-down houses. She turned, ducking into the alley as if she had just remembered where she was heading. If the guards were watching her, they would think she was forgetful instead of sneaking around. The alley between the business stalls and the houses was only big enough for two people to walk side by side. The putrid scent of offal and Goddess knew what else pervaded her senses. Discarded parchments, half eaten vegetables, torn cloth and even the dead carcass of a rabbit lined the sides of the alley. She ran her hands along the walls of the hovels, feeling the cracks and holes in the warped wooden boards. Each door was painted a different color, making it easier for the townspeople to distinguish them.

Hearing footsteps behind her, she cringed. Two scrawny teenage boys made their way into a flaky yellow painted door she had just passed. They paused, watching her closely. The lankier of the two elbowed his partner and motioned in her direction. Tugging on her cloak hood once more, her eyes flashed black, the shadows around her face grew deeper, and she watched as both boys stiffened and stepped through the yellow door. With a relieved snort, she wrapped her cloak tighter around her shoulders, fighting the urge to run all the way back to Garia. She needed safety. She needed protection. Shaking her head, she clenched her hands and continued towards the red painted door she had been told to look for. A tall gaunt man who looked greasy from head to toe propped up the wall next to the door.

"Yer late!" he growled angrily. Anna's gaze took in his tattered clothes, his missing teeth, his limp hair, and she shuddered. Everyone in this town looked as if they were starving. Thank Gaia she was rescuing at least some of them. She flashed him her most daring smile before sliding closer to his sweaty body.

"Late is a relative term..." she purred in her silkiest voice, her eyes flashing yet again. The shadows from the businesses behind them deepened. The man's eyes narrowed even more as she glanced over her shoulder. "I could have been on time with the King's Guard right behind me. I can still grab them if you would prefer..."

"I'd of preferred not doin' business wit ya, witch..." he grumbled as he opened the red smeared door. She stepped past him, making sure not to touch him and allowed her eyes to adjust to the dimness of the interior. The dirt floor was slightly cleaner than the outside alleyway. Tattered clothing was piled up in the corners. There were two filthy dirty cots against the far wall with no blankets and no sheets. Anna spied a small chest on one side and two very rickety looking chairs. "This brat here..." the man pointed to a young boy who stubbornly held the hand of a younger girl. "He's showin' signs..."

"Why hello there!" Anna trilled softly. She knelt down in front of the two children, pulling her hood back off her head. The young boy gasped as he looked at her. For a moment, but only a moment, that stung like it always did. She fingered the scar with a derisive smile. The angry red puckered skin slashed through her right eyebrow, across her eye, down the side of her nose and across her cheek to the back of her jaw. The scar itself could have taken her eye sight, but thankfully it only skimmed the upper lid, making a dotted line down her face. It was easy to hide in the cloak hood since no one could see much but the tip of her nose and her jaw. Anna gave the boy a friendly smile and held her hands out palm up. "I am not evil...and I promise I won't hurt you."

"You are very pretty." The little girl said in a shy voice, half seen from behind the boy's back. "Did it hurt?"

"Oh Gaia, yes, very much so." Anna gently rubbed the scar again, not remembering how she had received it or how it had hurt. Something as ugly and prominent as it was, had to have hurt, right? She shrugged off the feeling of forgetting something important. "But that was in the past and thank you for telling me I am pretty. Now, let me introduce myself. I am Anna Forsooth. And who might you two little lovelies be?"

"I am Jakob and this is Aria."

"What lovely names!" Anna clapped her hands. The man behind her growled and pushed her on her rump with his booted foot.

"Get on wit it. Ya don't need flummery. Quickly, afore the guards come checkin.'"

"Sir..." she said with barely contained rage. "It will take as long as it takes. I'll remind you to keep your body parts off me." Her eyes flashed quickly with an inner black light and the man immediately straightened, he turned towards the open door, and stepped outside. "Now." She turned her gaze back to the two children. "I heard that you, Jakob, might be showing signs of runes."

"I'll not be taken without my sister!" he cried, tears starting to stream down his face. "I can't protect her if I am not here." He whirled to the side and wrapped his sister up in a tight embrace. Anna felt her heart rip in two as the tears on Aria's face made little white paths through the grime on her cheeks. She reached out and bopped his nose with her finger.

"Silly goose. I would no sooner ask you to leave your sister unprotected than I would ask you to give up your rune craft. There are so few of us left in the world..."

"But momma said..." Aria sniffled as she peeked out from behind her big brothers' arms.

"Momma doesn't seem to be here..." Anna glanced around at the empty room. "And, if your brother is showing signs, I am sure in a few more years, you will as well. Now, we do have to work a little more quickly in case the guards come to check out the alley. I need you to let go of your sister and step forward Jackob. I need to see what we have here."

"It...it...won't...hurt..." he stuttered as he released his sister haltingly and pushed her a step away.

"My lovely young one..." Anna chuckled softly. "There are a lot of things in this world that will hurt, but my power isn't one of them. One more step closer and if you will take my hand..."

Jakob reached out a tentative hand and caught hers. He immediately relaxed, the fear and the anxiety slipping away as if he hadn't a care in the world. Anna's eyes flashed again with black light, the room seemed to buzz with energy, the shadows becoming deeper and darker, and then, just as quickly, she released his hand. The boy stood there momentarily stunned, then smiled brightly. Anna motioned for the little girl to step forward and she repeated the process. A large smile split the girl's lips as soon as Anna released her hand. There were shuffling sounds outside, alerting Anna to the fact that her unwitting watch dog was stirring. Either the guards were coming or he was shaking off her suggestion. She grabbed both of the children's hands and moved quickly to the door.

"I'm taking them both."

"But..." The man started to argue. His eyes glazed over black for a moment and then he stepped away, resuming his position against the wall. "The guards are coming...be quick."

Anna didn't need him to tell her to be quick. The idea of being caught and tossed into the Corrupt King Braun's dungeon was enough to make her hustle. At least as fast as she could with two children attached to either hand. She had made it just to the end of the alleyway when a guard grabbed her by the shoulder. She whirled to face him, anger seething through her body. The man flinched back when he saw her face, but didn't release her shoulder. He was wearing black boots, black leather breeches, an orange tunic and a black vest that declared him a royal guard. The man had shoulder length brown hair, big brown eyes, and a harsh glare that creased his forehead.

"What is the meaning of this?" she demanded. Anna hesitated, returning the guards scrutiny. He looked familiar, very familiar. Like the morning dew, the familiarity vanished, leaving her off balance.

"You'll need to come with me lady," the guard bellowed in a deep masculine voice.

"My children and I are going to the market. Is there a reason you are impeding us?"

"You need to come with me, witch!" he growled, he reached out to catch her arm.

"Unhand me you pigheaded fool." Anna let go of the two children, daring to use her rune casting just lightly enough to send the two little ones scattering in opposite directions.

Jakob and Aria took off, sending chickens fluttering, rabbits scurrying, and dogs scampering out of their path. Anna reached up and pulled her hood back over her head. Her best bet to evading capture would be to disappear into the crowd of people in the village market. She pushed through people, shoving one direction and then the other. Women with baskets of goods over their arms would bristle with indignation, men barely moved as her body hurtled into them, children only turned and watched as she cut through their midst. She had just made it to the far end of the stalls where she had purchased her breakfast. The white-haired old man was perched precariously on a rickety stool, watching as she darted through the throng of early morning shoppers. He raised an arm, his face tormented, shouting a warning to stop. It was too late. Her body slammed into an impenetrable wall of muscle.

Arms that were like steel bands immediately wrapped around her body, cutting off any chance of escape. Anna trailed her gaze up from the stark white clad chest to the well-trimmed black and silver beard. Her eyes finally fastening on those deep dark brown eyes that were framed with thick lashes. She felt her heart stop in her chest, her breath wheezed, her heart started tripping extra fast, and that sense of familiarity ripped through her once again. She pushed against the man and tried to free herself when the red-faced guard that had been chasing her came to a halt behind them. The man unwrapped his arms from her body and grabbed her wrist. He used his free hand to flick the gray hood off her face. Like most people, his gaze immediately went to the bright ugly puckered scar, trailing it from the start of her hairline to the end of her jaw, but he didn't flinch, only scoured her face for what seemed like an eternity. His gaze flicked to the crumbling poster on the tree she had studied that morning. Those dark brown eyes to ignited with recognition.

"She...she's..."

"Mikal..." the man holding her said with a bored yawn, shifting towards the slightly shorter man. "When you have caught your breath..."

Mikal bent over, gasping in several deep racking breaths and then stood straight. "She was approached...in the alley...with...two children."

"Really?" The man gave her another frank appraisal. His gaze paused at the flare of her hips, the swell of her chest, her wide doe eyes, the long unfettered brown curls of hair. "This woman," he snarled, his lip rising in disgust. "She attempted to abduct those two children? For what reason?"

"Rune caster..." Mikal gasped once more. He motioned to the other guard behind him. This guard was a blonde woman who pulled Aria and Jakob over to the quickly growing assortment of people. "Astrid narrowed in on them just as they exited a building. It has to be them, Your Highness. We tested the only other person in the alley and he is ordinary."

Anna risked looking up at King Braun. There were butterflies taking up residence in her gut. She knew this man and this guard; she just couldn't put her finger on where or why. Braun's grip on her wrist tightened to an even more painful hold. "Did you attempt to steal these children away?" She didn't answer, only narrowed her eyes, standing as straight as she could. "Who are these children to you? Answer me, witch!" he snapped as he shook her arm. Her teeth rattled inside her head and she lost her focus.

"Aria!" a woman screeched. Her feet churning up dirt clouds on the arid ground as she ran down the village market. Her clothes were so tattered that one more rip would surely render them useless. She stopped in front of the children, dropped to her knees and clutched the little girl in her arms. "This woman was trying to steal my child!" she accused. Anna tilted her head and raised a brow at the woman as she backed away from Jakob with Aria clutched in her arms.

"Astrid..." Braun growled. The woman's eyes flashed yellow and her hand dipped into a bag at her waist. She shook her head slightly, watching as the two disappeared. Those faint yellow flashes over her eyes happened twice more, once as Astrid looked at Jakob, and then again as she looked at Anna.

"Mikal!" Braun hollered as he thrust Anna away. "Take this witch and that child to the castle for sentencing."

"But she..." Mikal ground out as he motioned to the hand drawn picture on the tree. He saw the look King Braun shot in his direction and began wrapping ropes around Anna's wrists.

"Yes Mikal." King Braun smirked, crossing his arms over his chest and glancing between the woman and Mikal. "I think it is pretty obvious that she is the rune caster from Garia come to take the child across the border. They are both guilty of being rune casters. Take them to the castle at once. And Mikal!"

"Yes, King Braun," Mikal responded, dipping his head.

"Don't question my orders again."

"Of course, King Braun."

Chapter Two

Anna watched Braun mount a pure black stallion. He turned from the market without another glance. So, that was Corrupt King Ben Braun, the most feared man on the continent. Her eyes stayed on his broad back as he rode off. That niggling notion that she knew him and had watched him ride off once before fluttered through her brain. She was yanked harshly towards a cinnamon-colored horse. Jakob was sitting atop a beige mare, his body pinned against Astrid as she kicked the beast forward. Anna inhaled, feeling the pure terror undulating off of Jakob in waves. Using her power once more, she sent calming thoughts to Jakob as Mikal tied a lead to her bound hands and then to the saddle horn, leaving just enough slack for her to walk next to his horse.

This wasn't the first time Anna had been caught by guards in Enderton, but it was the first time she had been caught by the King's Guard. She prayed to Gaia that she wasn't executed. She struggled against the ropes on her wrist, hoping they would loosen, but Mikal was a clever guard. The ropes were tied just tight enough to keep her from getting loose, but were also loose enough not to damage her wrists. The walk back to the castle was long and exhausting. The heat of the day was causing rivulets of sweat to run down her body under the cloak. Her simple brown peasant dress was drenched by the halfway point to the castle. She stumbled over a branch and fell onto her face; a rock slicing her cheek. She heard Mikal curse softly and pull the horse to a stop. They rested for a few minutes, him giving her a sip of water from his canteen while he rested the horse. Then they packed back up and headed towards the castle once more. It seemed to take forever to arrive, but maybe that was because Anna was already exhausted.

Her first glimpse of Enderton Castle had her gaping like a fish. The castle was huge compared to the Garian castle. The stone structure was at least five levels high. There were three towers. The one on the left and right were slightly shorter than the one directly behind the forecourt. The stable in the forecourt was large enough for ten horses. There was a small castle market. There were tents set up along the guard walls with tables. People stood behind the tables and shouted at the people passing to buy their wares. Anna was pulled further into the throng of people. The castle proper was just behind another wall, this one slightly shorter than the guard wall. The castle proper held another stable. There was a forge set up to the left of the portcullis. Just behind the forge, soldiers and guards were training and sparring. To the right was a beautiful garden that had lilacs, lavender, sweetpeas and climbing vines of jasmine flowers. There was a small gazing pond with a stone bench. She spied a bed of hyacinths and hydrangeas planted around a miniature apple tree. She was untied from the horse as Mikal handed the reins off to the stable hand. She was yanked unceremoniously into the castle foyer. There were gold fixtures, luxurious wooden doors, tapestries made of the finest silks hanging from the walls, even the floor was hand cut marble, a luxurious hand-woven rug protecting it.

If the foyer was opulent, the main reception hall was even more so. This room was immaculate. It had gilt framed pictures hanging on the wall, showing the lineage of the kingdom. She noticed that the benches were padded with blue velvet. The walls were covered in long sheets of blue silk, tied near the middle with blue velvet ropes. The windows were set up high to let in light, but not enough to see. There were braziers at the end of each row of benches, making the room bright with light. Braziers were set on each side of the bench seats. The fires within those braziers cast flickering light through the room. Anna flinched, knowing that it would be hot, but was surprised when she walked down the middle aisle and felt no extra heat. Either they had figured out a way to make fire without heat, or they were using some sort of rune caster to create the light. She pondered this as Mikal escorted her towards the dais.

The crowds of seated people all turned and watched her slowly shuffle along. Anna would have expected the people to be all high-born nobles, but she was shocked to see the crowd held just as many peasants. She turned and focused her gaze on the dais. There was a large jewel encrusted golden throne with velvet blue cushions. From this distance, Anna guessed the jewels in the throne were diamonds. There was a smaller throne just to the right of the large one. It too was made of gold but had no jewels. The dais was curtained with more blue satin that hung down behind the thrones. To either side of the area was another set of braziers, lit with the heatless light. She was brought to a halt at the bottom step of the dais. Jakob was already there, Astrid holding him in place with her hands on his shoulder. Anna squared her shoulders and waited, her gaze shifting about to take in the splendor of the room. Not only was Braun the Corrupt King, he was an extravagant one at that. He obviously spent his riches and cared nothing for his people.

"Mikal!" a man bellowed. Anna shifted her eyes towards the voice. Braun walked out from behind the throne and settled down onto his blue velvet cushion. His glaring white tunic making her eyes water.

"Your highness. These two are being charged as rune casters."

"The child has no power!" Anna snapped. "Let him go."

"The child has no power?" King Braun chuckled with mirth and tilted his head, his fingers of his left hand rubbed gently at his beard. "One has to wonder, then, what you were doing stealing two children from the market. What was your true intent?"

"He has no power!" she growled. "Send him back to his mother."

"His mother? And who would that be?"

"The woman from the market."

Braun stared at the woman in front of him. She was covered from head to toe in dirt and bruises. Her dress and cloak had seen much better days. She was half starved, but somewhere under all that, she stirred something primal inside of him. For a brief moment, images of what he wanted to do with her engulfed his mind, his eyes flashing white. He shook his head, trying to rid himself of those images, and glanced at Mikal. He had to suppress his powers better. It had been a very long time since he had released his power. "If that woman was mother to both children, why did she only take the girl?"

Anna turned her head, wondering if she should try using her power to influence the King. She could feel Jakob trembling next to her. His fear and anxiety pooled in her stomach, her own fear choked her throat, she pushed Braun with her mind, suggesting that he let them go. "He has no powers. I promise you! Just let him go...you have me."

"So, you would rather be tried as a child abductor than a rune caster?" King Braun heard the court chuckle. "No harm will come to the child. I can promise that. Astrid..."

Anna attempted to grab Jakob and run from the room, but Mikal was prepared for that. He caught her arms and pulled her back into his chest, holding her tight. With all the strength she could muster, she raised her foot and slammed it down on his. He dropped one hand only, holding her with the other as he hopped up and down, cussing and cursing. The moment would have been comical if the situation hadn't been so dire. Anna felt a prickle in her brain. A flutter of something trying to rise to the surface. That moment of almost remembering something important. There was a second when her eyes connected with the Corrupt King's and he was smirking as if he knew what she couldn't remember. The moment passed and Mikal eventually pulled her back into his grasp, his foot only twitching slightly.

Astrid waited until they finally settled down before pulling out a large three-inch sphere of crystal. She pressed the small ball against Jakob's brow, right between his eyes. Astrid's eyes flashed yellow once more, the room darkened for a moment, but then the room flooded with pale blue light. Images of water in all stages and forms flashed through the light. The scent of rain filled her nose. Damn, whatever Astrid did with that crystal, she was good. Anna had never seen anyone use a crystal to do this. She briefly wondered how it worked and if she would be able to counter it. The crowded room began to mutter. Mikal reached over and clasped a bracelet around Jakob's wrist and immediately the light went out. Reaching out tentatively with her power, Anna could not feel Jakob's power any longer. Strangely enough though, she could feel several other rune casters in the room. Without touching them, she couldn't know who they were, but they were there. How could a man who hated rune casters have so many in his court room?

"What is your name child?" King Braun demanded, bringing the attention of the room back to him.

"Jakob."

"Your family name," he commanded.

"Trentwood."

"Jakob Trentwood, you are hereby declared a rune caster and as such you are sentenced to death. Guards, take him to the dungeon. Astrid..." King Braun motioned towards Anna. "Show us what her rune craft is..."

"I have none..." Anna replied defiantly, struggling against Mikal's grip.

Astrid held the same crystal up to Anna's brow. The cool stone felt welcome against her sweaty brow. For a very long moment nothing happened. Anna was focused on wrapping her power up into a tight bundle deep down inside. The sharp cracking sound made everyone gasp as the crystal broke in half, falling uselessly from Astrid's hand. Anna smirked in triumph.

"Well!" King Braun demanded. He watched as Astrid fumbled in her pouch at her waist.

"My apologies, Your Highness. This one is extremely strong. She is hiding her power fairly well."

"You show me her power Astrid, or I will lock you up in the dungeon as well!" he bellowed.

"Yes, Your Highness." Astrid dipped a curtsy before seizing another ball from her pouch.

This crystal was twice the size of the first. She placed it against Anna's brow and hissed as the room flooded with shadows. No corner of the room was left untouched. Images of everything flooded through the room, there were trees, water, animals, people, rocks, grass, and mountains. The images just kept scrolling, one replacing another. The scent of flowers, water, loamy soil, and rocks invaded her olfactory. Anna closed her eyes and bowed her head with defeat. She was dead. The room was exceptionally quiet. She turned a challenging gaze to the king. He was sitting back in his seat, his eyes burning a hole through her as he thought, a small wrinkle in his brow the only sign he was attentive at all. Astrid dropped the crystal back in her pouch and stepped away from Anna.

"What is your name?" the King asked, tilting his head slightly and leaning forward.

"Anna..." she quivered, although she wasn't sure if it was in fear, attraction, or the strange recollection that hovered just on the edge of her memory.

"Anna what?"

"Anna Forsooth." She watched his eyes widen with recognition, understanding filling his gaze. He sat back, steeling his face to show no emotion as the crowded room erupted in a roar of shouts. Mikal snapped a bracelet around her wrist and she lost connection to her power. The world become slightly dimmer and grayer to her eyes.

"Anna Forsooth, you are hereby declared a rune caster and as such you are sentenced to death. Guards, take her to the dungeon."

Anna shuddered as Mikal caught her arms and dragged her physically out of the room. She felt the first hint of fear fluttering in her chest. She had to be strong. She couldn't allow herself to go to pieces or give up. She needed to find a way out of this. She needed to protect Jakob if she could. She kept her eyes peeled as she was marched deep down below the castle. The halls she walked through were lined on either side with cells. Each cell contained a floor of straw, a single wooden bucket, and a wooden board bolted onto the wall for a cot. The cells slowly became darker, the walls growing damp, the smell of mold and mildew getting stronger as they walked. There were a few torches set into the wall, casting just enough light to grant them a safe passage.

After passing fifty cells, Mikal turned her left at the end of the hall, moving through a solid metal door with a small peep hole. The passage she walked through was pitch dark. She shuffled her feet, feeling slimy moss under her worn boots. She heard a few muffled groans, coughs, and wheezes as she was pushed to move faster. Just when she thought she wouldn't make it much farther, Mikal caught her arm, stopping her. There was a metallic click and then a grating noise as he swung open yet another heavy metal door. This one didn't have a peep hole, just a large padlock.

Anna struggled against Mikal once more, but he was stronger than she would ever be. She found herself blinking in confusion as she was thrust into a brightly lit room. Unlike the previous mile of hallways, this room was roughly hewn from the bedrock. It had braziers along the walls at about every six feet, all lit and glowing brightly with that heatless flame. The room was large enough to house the trial they had just undergone. Jakob was standing in the middle of the room between five pillars of stone. Each pillar was around four feet off the ground and each held one large iron ring facing the center. There were dark rusty stains on the rocks below where Jakob was. He ran to her and wrapped his arms around her legs, tears streaming down his little face. She dropped to her knees, finally pulling out of Mikal's iron grip. Mikal unbound her wrists, making her reel slightly in shock. She stood, wrapping Jakob tighter against her, and whispering assurances that everything would be fine.

"Anna Forsooth and Jakob Trentwood," Astrid said with a suppressed grin. "King Braun has decreed that no rune caster shall live within the borders of Enderton. Use of rune casting is a crime against the crown. Both of you have been proven to be rune casters. Therefore, it has been proclaimed that you will die for these crimes." Astrid paused, motioning to someone behind her. A horse was brought into the room. Anna shuddered. Seems they were to be drawn and quartered. Not exactly the punishment she would have picked. She was prodded into the circle of stones where Jakob had stood earlier.

"Your new name shall now be Justin Briarpatch." Astrid ripped Jakob from Anna's grasp.

"No!" Anna shouted, trying to get him back. She clawed and kicked as much as she had strength for. Mikal only sucked on his teeth, grabbing her arms and pinning her tightly to his chest.

"Put the ropes on again if you must," King Braun commanded as he strode into the brightly lit room. The walls seemed to brighten even more with his presence. Anna turned her tear-streaked face towards him, flicking her power out. There were rumors that King Braun was a powerful rune caster himself, all Anna had to do was reach his power. Nothing. She was looking at an ordinary. "Justin Briarpatch..." he turned his attention to the child in Astrid's arms. "Jakob Trentwood is now dead. You, Justin, must go to Garia now. You must stay in Garia until you are strong, trained, and I call for you to return. Do you understand?"

"Yes..." Jakob mewled pathetically. Tears ran rivers down his face as he pushed his lower lip out in a confused pout. "So, I am not dying???"

"Not today my child, and hopefully not for a very long time. I need your power to grow big and strong to help protect my kingdom. Go Justin, and return to me a strong warrior!"

Astrid mounted the beige-colored horse that was waiting near the large opening in the back wall. With one final glance at the King, she spurred the horse and took off out into the open courtyard. Anna stood, mouth agape, body trembling, hands shaking. She turned her eyes and glanced back at King Braun. Her arms were still being held by Mikal. Thank Gaia for that, for without him, she would have fallen down in total shock. What in the rune points had just happened? King Braun leaned against the wall, arms crossed over his vivid white tunic, legs crossed at his immaculate booted ankles. He assessed her from the top of her brown headed hair to the bottoms of her feet. She returned the stare, feeling her cheeks heat lightly.

"Your highness...she is..."

"I know who she is, Mikal." King Braun rubbed his face in weariness. "But as you can see, she doesn't know who she is. Which makes this all the more...complicated."

"What are we going to do with her?"

Anna turned her gaze to Mikal, and thrust her power out. Nothing happened. She yanked her arm, only causing Mikal to grunt. When she turned her head back, she gasped, as King Braun was standing in front of her. He caught her chin and held her face, looking down into her eyes. A spark of passion flared in her gut as his eyes flared white, his finger traced the cut on her left cheek, then the scar on her right cheek. She inhaled deeply, catching his scent of spice, man and leather. It was an intoxicating combination, pushing that shimmer of passion forcefully to the front of her mind. She watched as his eyes flashed white once more. He had to be a rune caster. She didn't know any ordinary whose eyes flashed like that.

"This one is going to be more complicated." King Braun sighed and released her face from his grip. "I can release her to Garia as I did with Jakob, but she will just keep returning to steal all the caster children and smuggle them back to Garia for King Mawhorter. I don't think I have the energy today to convince her to work for my side. It took us a long time to find her." He glanced at Mikal, seeing his eager face. "It has been twenty years. I'd hate to miss the chance to rekindle our acquaintance, even if she is reluctant and ignorant."

Twenty years? Surely, she wasn't that woman on the awkwardly drawn brittle parchment in the market. How in the world could anyone recognize that woman from that picture? If he was truly the one looking for her, wouldn't she remember him? She did feel that small moment of whispering memory. Naw, she only resembled the strange woman. He was desperate and grasping at straws. The longer he thought he knew her, the longer she could stay alive.

"Take Anna to the purple suite upstairs. Send the maids to give her a good scrub down. Maize to care to her wounds and bruises. Maybe even Juta..." he paused, sizing her up and down once more. "Yes, Juta can get her a wardrobe together."

"Very well, your highness..." Mikal hooted in triumph as he yanked her out of the underground arena.

Chapter Three

The purple room was indeed purple. Every shade of purple was reflected somewhere in the room. The hand braided rugs over the stone floor were a pale lavender and a deep grape. The curtains around the floor to ceiling windows were majestic mountain purple. The walls had been painted with a shade of orchid. Anna focused on the bed, suddenly feeling the weariness inside her bones. The bedcover on the hand-carved and lightly stained four poster bed was a dark eggplant, trimmed with satin piping of a vivid amethyst.

A very short stocky woman with long braided blonde hair and gray eyes was holding audience in the room. The woman pointed and grunted at different things and other women moved quickly to that item without question, knowing exactly what to do. Anna felt her body relax slightly as Mikal disappeared, closing the door behind him. While she wasn't bound with ropes, she was sure he was on the other side of the door. Anna gravitated toward the two plum colored wing back chairs with periwinkle satin pillows that were framing the fireplace. Her body was bone tired. She had no more fuel. She eased herself into a sitting position, her bottom almost touching the plush seat, then was yanked off balance by a pair of tiny dwarven hands.

"Zura..." the woman snipped, shoving Anna towards a screen at the back of the room just behind the bed.

Anna noted with some appreciation that the castle had been updated with modern conveniences like plumbing. The steam coming off the tub told her that the water was being heated in some way. Without too much argument, Anna allowed the two women to scrub her down with the lavender scented soap. A yawn crept up through her soul as they plucked her now clean body from the water and began to roughly towel her dry. She was wrapped in a separate dry towel and then shuffled back to the main room where another woman took her hands. This woman was a lovely shade of cocoa with black hair she kept cut short to her scalp. Her almond shaped eyes were a rare shade of green, bordering on teal. Anna watched as her eyes flashed with a soft blue glow and her cuts and bruises began to disappear.

Enderton Castle was a very bizarre enigma. King Braun proclaimed no rune casters should be allowed to live in his kingdom, and yet here was a rune caster using her powers under the assumption of King Braun's request. Anna stifled another yawn when the woman named Maize finally dipped her head, turned, and left without much to say. Not being able to feel Maize's power as she worked was a little unsettling. Anna's eyes strayed to the bracelet on her wrist. It was about two inches wide, stamped with Rune like symbols, and pulsed with a soft white glow. She tried to pry the cuff off, disguising her movements as if she was scratching an itch. It was no use. The bracelet wouldn't budge. The short dwarven woman approached and shooed her to the side of the bed where several outfits had been laid out. Tiredly Anna glanced out one of the large windows. The sun was just now hitting the horizon, meaning it was evening meal time. She let out a tired sigh, eyeing the heavenly cloud of comfort the bed offered instead.

"You...dress..." the dwarven woman commanded in the common tongue, poking Anna in her ribs and then pointing at the simple gowns.

The gowns were done up in Garian style which suited her just fine. The top of the dress had cap sleeves and gathers around the low neck. The fabric was then belted around the waist and fell to just around her ankles. Anna reached for the one closest to her without thinking. It was a russet brown, with a black belt. She snapped her hand back in surprise when the dwarf woman smacked her hand. A few dwarven curses later, a black Garian gown was shoved into her hands. There was nothing exciting about the dress, other than it was finely made and of the smoothest cotton she had ever felt. There was no embroidery, no embellishment, and no lace. It was the best outfit she had ever seen, except for two holes around her hips on either side. The seamstress must have missed those areas when she put the dress together. The short woman thrust a corset of pure white into her hands and Anna dropped it on the bed. This part of Garian fashion she had refused since she was old enough to voice her opinion. She had no need for such a contraption.

"I will not put that horrible restrictive invention on!" Anna answered, crossing her arms over her chest.

"Yes...immodest."

"No. I will not."

"Yes!" Juta crossed her arms, her stance becoming wider, her nostrils flaring. She opened her mouth to issue another command but stopped when another voice floated through the door.

"Anna..." a very masculine timbre answered from the other side of the purple room door. She straightened her spine, her eyes narrowing when she recognized the King's voice and that the door was half open. "You will put on whatever Juta tells you to. It is getting late and I am exhausted. If we have to fight any more, I will personally come into that room and dress you myself! Do you understand?"

"No..." Anna shifted her gaze to Juta and gulped. "Has he been outside that door the whole time?" Juta nodded with a smile and wicked cackle. "Oh, Goddess me...what in the rune points...yes *King* Braun!" she growled.

"Do you really think that necessary?" she demanded, fixing Juta with a black look and crossing her arms over her chest in defiance. "I mean, I am hardly fat enough to require it."

"The corset is for modesty...and style." She said haltingly in the common tongue and loudly enough to carry out the door. "If you refuse again..."

Anna's eyes widened as King Braun growled and stormed into the room. He took the corset from Juta's hands and wrapped it around Anna's tiny waist. There was a seven-inch gap even after it was cinched up. Anna squeezed her eyes shut. Her cheeks growing red with embarrassment. The feel of the King's hands as they brushed against her arms and waist sent shivers along her nerves, her mind taking those brushes to a more heated ending. Anna waited for him to cinch the laces and be done with her, but he was sharing a look with Juta who was jotting down notes on a piece of parchment. He tugged the corset off and tossed it onto the bed.

Juta dropped a pair of tiny lady slippers down in front of her. Braun crossed his arms and stared Anna down until she slipped her feet into them. Juta continued to walk around her making notes. She tucked a strand of Anna's hair behind her ear, tugged on the skirt here, tucked something in there, as if Anna was a statue to be rearranged for her delight. The King held Anna's eyes and quickly she felt her body warm even more. There was lightning in those eyes. She should look away. This man was the devil. He was damned. He was despicable. He was cursed. He was smoldering hot. She opened her mouth, needing more air than she was getting. He raised one black eyebrow as he watched her reaction, his eyes flashing white. Juta finally sucked her teeth and motioned for her to leave the room.

Braun turned to Anna and gave her a half smirk. "Now that you are dressed appropriately and not covered in head-to-toe filth, shall we have dinner before bed?"

"Bed?" she squeaked. He was close enough she could smell the spice, leather, and horse scent that clung to him. "Whose bed?"

"Your bed...and mine, separately." He chuckled as he pushed the door open and stepped into the hall. There were four guards standing outside the door. Each was equipped with a sword, a dagger, and what appeared to be a mace. She scrambled after him, too tired to attempt an escape and too hungry to fight. "Relax Anna, I am not going to ravage you on the first night."

They walked an extremely short distance. The hall ended and turned left. They walked another short distance to a door which he opened without knocking. Her eyes widened as she spied a vaguely remembered study. Letting out a heavy breath, she followed him inside. To the right of the door was a large ornately hand carved wooden desk with a large blue velvet lined wing back chair with gold braiding. There were two smaller wooden chairs with blue velvet cushions directly in front of the desk. On the wall behind all of this were floor to ceiling bookshelves. The shelves were filled with books, trinkets, statues, even a dagger was stabbed at a jaunty angle in front of some books. Anna itched to look through the titles, gaze at the trinkets, memorize the lines of the statues. Her mother always said you could judge a person by what they hold most dear. She had a feeling from how full those bookcases were that Braun held a lot near and dear to him. There were two doors directly across from the door they had just entered through. She watched as Braun disappeared into the first one. He didn't command her to follow and no light appeared so she hung back, tracing her hands along the shelf of a bookcase and pausing on the life like marble sculpture of an older man.

Anna's brain spasmed as a tiny corner of the fog lifted. She could see this man growling about his son's misguided affections. Her eyes strayed to the dagger stabbed into the shelf just three paces from her. That very same dagger had sliced her skin just under her hair line, across her nose and down her jaw. Pain filled her as she struggled, watching the demented old man as he sliced down her face. The knife skidded to one side and then the other as she struggled against him. A tear slipped down her cheek as she shuddered from the memory. She turned, deciding she didn't need to look at any more items right now when her hand brushed a small wooden carving. She recognized her own clumsy work. It had been an attempt at carving a monkey out of a piece of white ash. It wasn't a very good carving, in fact, she couldn't even tell that it was a monkey, but it was definitely something she had worked. Curiously, she worked her way over to the left side of the room.

There was a large wooden table that covered most of the room. It had a hand carved map of the continent. The mountains were high, the trees were rough and the waters were smooth on this carving. She marveled at the craftsmanship, running her fingers lightly along the inlaid white stone that marked the border. She noted the position of several black markers, a raised brow her only reaction. If Braun was going to war with Garia, those markers should be on Garian territory, not on Enderton. Unless he was under attack from Garia. There was a soft sound of a door closing and she turned to the two doors. Braun had opened the second door on that wall and was standing in front of it, bootless, shirtless, his hair mused. Anna found herself gaping at the finely sculpted torso, noting the parallel scars on his left shoulder, the pink and paling scar just above his right hip. She swallowed hard as she watched the flex of his muscles as he motioned for her to join him. Bloody rune points, she had to keep her gaze on his face or she wouldn't remember that she needed to escape. Anna stepped lightly around him and into a small private dining area.

The table was already set for two although it could hold six. She noticed one place setting at each end of the table and gladly settled into the chair closest to the door. Braun of course took the opposite side to keep his eye on the coming and goings from his study. She marveled at the simplicity of this room. The table was a simple construction of wood, buffed to a high shine. The trenchers were wood instead of silver or gold. The goblets they drank from were also wooden and polished to a high shine. There were simple cotton linens on the table, a simple meal of vegetable broth, and what tasted of apple juice in her cup. The room was such a simple design for a King. It should have been gilt, carved, and jewel encrusted. Instead, it was something you would find in a woodworker's home. She felt a little more at peace here in his private chamber as she lifted a wooden spoon and tucked into the broth.

"What do you plan to do with me?" she demanded. Her body growled in response to the white flash of his eyes and her cheeks flushed. She pushed it away, focusing only on putting food in her mouth, even if that food tasted about the same as the carrots from this mornings' breakfast.

"How long have you gone without eating Anna?" he replied, ignoring her question.

"I had a carrot this morning."

"That half rotten thing we found in your cloak?" He chuckled, eating a chunk of fresh warm bread. "What did you have before that?"

"Whatever I could scavenge from the woods."

"So, you haven't had much to eat in the last few weeks..." he motioned to someone just behind her and she jumped as an arm reached around and settled another trencher with the most delectable smelling chicken on it. "You need your strength. Eat the chicken."

"Is it poisoned?" she asked, narrowing her eyes and sniffing the meat.

"It wouldn't matter if it was..." he finished his meal and leaned back against his chair. "Do you know what your power is?"

"Not really...but does it really matter" Anna answered honestly. She took a bite of the chicken, savoring the taste, then took several more bites. It had been a long time since she had eaten meat. She noticed Ben watching her every movement. He watched as she used her spoon and knife to cut the chicken into smaller pieces. He watched as she delicately raised the goblet to her lips for a drink. It was becoming a very maddening meal.

"Yes, it does." He let out a heavy breath. "I have been looking for you for a very long time Anna. Your power will help save my kingdom. Not only that, but I have known you since we were young. You don't recognize me at all?"

"Nope..." Anna popped another piece of chicken in her mouth. "I would remember if I knew the Corrupt King. What exactly is my power and how can it save your kingdom? Did Garia go to war with you and I wasn't notified?"

"You are a black rune caster."

"Those are myths."

"No more so than a white rune caster."

"Those are a greater myth."

"Let's suspend reality for a moment." Ben raised a black eyebrow in her direction and smiled patiently. "Black rune casters are able to physically do anything the other rune casters can do. Mentally they are great at making suggestions that people follow. That cut on your left cheek from earlier, you could have healed it yourself. That scar across your face, you can get rid of it when you want. This is why you are so important to my kingdom. I need you to heal my land from a blight I created twenty years ago. My people are slowly starving to death."

"I already told you, white rune casting and black rune casting are myths. They don't exist." Anna harrumphed. She heaved a deep breath as he snatched the bracelet off her wrist.

Images of her body entwined with his on the dining table flooded through her mind. The room became brighter as she fought to free herself from the onslaught he was mentally casting. His mouth was savoring her skin as if she was the roasted chicken. Anna reeled back in her chair. Suddenly her thoughts were turned against her and she saw herself dropping into his lap, her fingers entwined in his black hair, her lips kissing him thoroughly. His hand swept under her skirts, stroking her thighs. She panted for air. There was no escape. Her body throbbed with her need. She was begging softly, her hands clutching at the linen table cloth, her mind trying to decide if she wanted him to follow through with the images or if she wanted him to stop.

She felt her power stir within her in response to her emotional overload. Tapping it, she plucked it like a string and forced it towards him, her eyes flashing black, the room growing darker. Instantly the barrage stopped. She slumped forward against the table; her energy completely used up. Then she was cut off from her power again. He had snapped the damn bracelet back on her wrist. Her eyes found his and he smirked. She hadn't been the only one affected by that power surge. His face was flushed, his eyes wide, and he was panting just as heavily as she was. He stood next to her at the end of the table, his hand raised. It moved towards her hair, then stopped. His fingers curled into his palm, then dropped back to his side.

"Tell me again how white rune casters don't exist...and I'll tell you again how you are a black rune caster." He stepped out of the private dining chamber. "Sleep well tonight, Anna."

Anna sat motionless as King Braun left the private dining chamber and disappeared behind the only other door in the study. She had to assume that was his private bed chamber. A guard cupped her elbow gently. She rose from the chair and followed him out, down the very short hallway. He thrust open the door to her new gilded cage and she walked inside. Juta stood just inside the door, hands clasped in front of her waist, her eyes trained on the wall. She didn't move until the door closed and the guard disappeared out of sight. The short dwarven woman hustled Anna back to a dressing stool where she helped Anna strip out of her clothes and tug on a black almost sheer nightgown. It was made of silk and clung to her body like a glove. Anna loved it, wondering why peasants were not allowed these types of luxuries. She sat obediently as Juta combed out her hair, mumbling odd little nothings in her native tongue. Anna yawned, hiding a smile behind her hand at some of them. Juta really had a fine grasp of curses and bawdy comments. Some of them were starting to make Anna blush. She stamped out a giggle, pretending to belch instead as Juta's sharp gray eyes caught hers in the looking glass on the dressing table.

Juta smacked her with the back of the silver handled brush on the shoulder and motioned her towards the bed. Anna crawled under the covers and sighed in bliss as the moss filled mattress hugged her tired body. She fell off into an almost instant sleep, dreams of a tall swarthy man taking liberties filling her mind. Juta watched Anna fall asleep and then bustled down the hallway to the King's study, knowing he would still be awake. She tapped softly on the door as a courtesy before barging into the room. The king was sitting at the desk, one leg looped around the arm of his chair, his arm resting on the armrest and propping his head up as he gazed across the room at the map of the kingdoms. Juta tossed her stack of parchments onto the desk and watched as his gaze finally focused on her.

"Will you be able to watch over her Juta, or do I need to assign a permanent maiden?"

"Ah...she is a wisp of a girl. I can handle her." Juta responded in her native dwarven tongue, waving her hand at his question as if it was silly and non-sense. "I worked these up during dinner. With your approval..."

Ben glanced through the parchments at the drawings she had created of the dresses she would sew. He gave her detailed instructions of other items he wanted crafted for her. Juta took notes and then retrieved her stack of parchments. Her eyes missed nothing, noting he had pulled a sketch out and hid it under a stack of books. As she closed the door to his study, she mumbled about sticky fingered elves getting retribution from her sharp tongue. Ben ignored her, turning back to his reverie. He pulled the drawing back out. It was a much better picture than the one he had done as a teenager. Anna was looking to the right, the scar on her face almost completely hidden. The gown showed off her lovely curves and her long legs, hiding nothing from his view. He sighed, dropping it into a drawer in his desk. He was in trouble with a capital T. Anna was the woman he had fallen in love with as a teenager. She was also the one who had caused his power to flare. She was the woman who had made him insane. She was also his last hope for his kingdom. He couldn't reverse what he had done twenty years ago, Goddess knew he had tried. The only chance he had was someone stronger than him, and Anna was the only one that had ever rejected his power. She had to be able to heal the blight. He had seen the hope that had filled Mikal's eyes this morning. He could only hope that she would eventually agree to help him. If she didn't, Garia was the only place left that could save them.

Chapter Four

"Wake up you lazy peasant!" Juta cried in dwarven, as she yanked the covers off Anna. Anna gurgled low in her throat, curling into a tighter ball as she rolled away from those harsh grasping hands. "The King demands you join him for breaking fast. Get up!"

"He can rot..." Anna moaned into a pillow, replying back in dwarven. Her body was still alive with her need for the man. It was almost as if his power was still working on her even after he slapped the bloody bracelet back on. She squeezed her eyes tight as she thought of his black hair, going just a tad silver around the temples. She wanted to run her fingers through it even now. Damn her traitorous body for even having those thoughts of the Corrupt King. She scratched her traitorous hands, still feeling the smooth silky texture of his hair. "I am too tired to get up, for Gaia's sake. I had a very trying day."

"How a peasant girl like you knows dwarven I will never know but you will be too sore in a moment. I will strip your hide myself if you don't get out of that bed!" Juta promised as she grabbed one of Anna's ankles and yanked.

There was the sound of the room's door opening and then Juta cackling in malicious glee. Anna cracked one eye open and peeked out from under her arm. Braun strode into the room. Damn him for looking as good as he did right now. Shockingly enough the man was wearing only a pair of black breeches. He walked to the side of the bed, reached down, grabbed Anna by the hips, and yanked her up as if she weighed nothing. He settled her onto her feet and pushed her towards Juta. Curses flew from her mouth as she was pushed behind the dressing area. The sheer nightgown was yanked off. Her hair was left braided, but tucked up into a bun at the nape of her neck. The small dwarven woman splashed cold water into Anna's face and listened to the mixed language cursing, giving back some of her own in dwarven as Anna was shoved into a pair of breeches and a much more unusual tunic.

Once done, Juta shoved her out from behind the privacy screen. Anna heard the sharp intake of breath from Braun and snapped her furious brown eyed gaze up to his. She smiled smugly. If she was still heated through from Ben's show of rune casting last night, her whole night of lustful dreams, and from this morning's traitorous thoughts, she was happy to see that favor returned ten-fold just by getting dressed. His cheeks and chest had reddened delightfully as his gaze stuck on her legs and hips. She crossed her arms over her chest, his gaze immediately moving to that area, watching the fabric strain against her breasts.

"Just as you requested, your highness." Juta remarked with a wide beaming smile. "She will have plenty of movement in these." Anna fidgeted with a hole in the seam of her breeches and sighed when Juta slapped her hands away. For being a royal seamstress, it seemed odd that Juta had missed something. She walked around Anna, preening like a peacock as she adjusted the fabrics. "Perfect fit if I say so myself..."

"Very good, Juta." Braun swallowed hard, watching Anna finger the small hole on the outside leg seam of her breeches. "She'll need several more of these..."

"Yes, your highness. I shall have my seamstress work them up as soon as she finishes her gowns for the week."

"Tell her to patch the holes in the seams as well..." Anna grumbled as she was forced non-physically from the room.

Braun only moved in her direction, forcing her to jump out of his way. She paused at the white wall of the hallway. She glanced up and down the stone floor. There were no guards watching her at the moment. She turned left out of her room instead of right, the opposite direction from the king's private chambers, and walked quickly down the hall to the next junction. A pair of guards materialized in front of her. Letting out a shaky laugh, Anna cursed under her breath as Braun caught up to her. He turned her left to the connecting hall, right down the next two halls and up a flight of stairs and into a large open room.

Anna was sure this room was used for dancing. The wooden floor gleamed under the flickering of lantern light. She spied a few floor-to-ceiling windows covered with white gauzy fabric and noticed that it was still pitch-black outside. Why the hell were they up before the sun? Braun turned in the middle of the room and motioned for her to join him. Along the outer wall in the very back, Anna spied wooden staffs. There seemed to also be a few wooden swords and the like. Ah, he had brought her to his indoor training area. She glanced down at the clothes she was wearing and felt her cheeks heat up. He was obviously going to make her work out, or kill her as he sparred with her, she wasn't sure which made more sense.

"That is a very lovely shade of red on you Anna." Braun laughed deeply at her blush. "Come here, I am not going to hurt you. I think you could benefit with a little training, nothing more."

"Training?" Anna stood next to him and watched as he moved into a very relaxed stance. "What sort of training?"

"Relaxation, control, rune casting, protection, those sorts of things. Follow my movements..." Anna followed his slow methodical movements. Her breathing slowed to match his after a while and she truly did feel as if her body was relaxing.

"Rune casting?" she asked, as she slowly got used to the routine. "For a King who has outlawed rune casting from his kingdom, why would you train me in that?" He moved into a jog around the dance hall floor and she followed, intent on knowing what made this man tick. One of the best ways for her to escape would be to know all she could about him and his kingdom.

"I may have directly forbidden it, but I am a rune caster myself. I can't deny my people who they are."

"Then why forbid it in the first place?"

"It's a strategic move that I had hoped not to have to put in place. I'm planning ahead for the future. If it doesn't happen, I will bring my people back to me." He stopped jogging, pulling her into a defensive position, ignoring the slight flare of heat as he touched her body. He showed her a few simple blocks and evades.

"And you think I have black rune casting...the ability to do everything and anything?"

"Anna..." he sighed, jabbing at her, then twisting to pull her into a hold. "I don't think you are a black rune caster." He released her from his grasp and took an aggressive stand. "I know you are a black rune caster. You've seen me when I use my power...what color do my eyes flash?"

"White..." she replied without hesitation. She evaded his gentle jab, ducked under his hold, and kicked out with her foot, catching him in the stomach. He woofed but didn't go down.

"And what color were Astrid's when she tested you and Jakob?"

"Yellow."

"Your eyes flash black when you cast. What colors have you seen others flash?"

Braun watched as the thoughts churned through her mind. He pulled them to a stop, holding her hands in his as it finally dawned on her. "The color your eyes flash is the color of your power? That is so neat! I never connected that. I always just looked inside them."

"Let's work on powers. You are excellent with your mental casting; I can give you that." He rubbed the back of his neck and gave her a sheepish grin. "Mikal!" he hollered. The door at the far back of the room opened and Mikal strode inside from the balcony. He gave a hallow bow to his King, then turned to her, his tunic unbuttoned, his boots slung over his shoulder, and his shoulder length brown hair was sticking out at weird angles.

"Don't worry kiddo..." he winked, dropping his boots onto the floor next to Braun. "I'll take it easy on you until you can get the hang of it."

"Exactly what are you training me to do?" she asked, narrowing her eyes and circling him as he moved in a circle around her.

"I'm going to expand your powers, get you used to casting. You use a mental deflection, the power of suggestion, right?"

"Sure..." she shrugged. "Never really thought about it much. I just think of what I want them to do and watch as they either do it or don't."

"Ah Goddess..." Mikal rolled his eyes and reached out with his power. "You know absolutely nothing about powers. We are going to have to start with remedial training...Your Highness."

"Whatever is necessary, Mikal." Ben stood with his arms crossed over his chest. "I trust you implicitly."

Anna stopped talking, and stopped moving. She could feel something happening to her. Even after spending a slightly sleepless night in a soft bed, she had risen, albeit against her will, feeling refreshed and energized. At this moment she was feeling that energy quickly draining away. She glanced at Mikal, dropped to a knee, kicked out and watched as he fell on the ground. She turned in shock as she heard the guffaws of Braun. Ben was laughing uncontrollably. Mikal rose to his feet, gawping at her in outrage, and she was feeling all of that energy quickly flooding back into her system. That slow feeling of de ja vu seeped back into her brain as she watched the king laugh at his guard. Another corner of the shrouded memory lifted and she suddenly knew without a doubt that these two were brothers. She studied Mikal a little closer and realized there was a family resemblance, she had chosen not to see it. Who would ever have thought that the King's brother would choose to be a guard? It was such a common and low-born position for a prince.

"Alright." Mikal crossed his arms over his chest. The fabric of his orange shirt gaped open, revealing a leather cord wrapped around a wooden carving.

Anna gasped as she recognized yet another one of her attempts at wood carving. This one was carved from cherry wood, giving the pig a slightly pink tint. The memory of brothers opened a little more and she remembered shoving the carvings into their hands, watching as they both tucked them into their breeches and then running off to the stables with them. She did know them, but was she really the person they remembered from so long ago, or was her meeting them a passing thing? They were dressed in frippery and her in her finest dress, so maybe they were at some social function where the peasants were allowed. She shook her head as Mikal's face lit up and he stepped forward, removing the silver cuff from her wrist. He tucked it in his pocket just as he had the pig around his neck when he was ten.

"My apologies. I'm going to assume you lashed out physically because you were still buffered. Let's try again, only this time, no physical attacking."

Anna felt her power flood back again and was relieved. The colors in the room brightened slightly. She again felt that drain on her energy. She flexed her mental power, reaching out to see Mikal's tight ball of orange. She mentally flicked it and watched as he began sputtering, his eyes widened and he dropped to one knee. She pulled her power back. Had she hurt him? Her energy began draining again quicker. She narrowed her eyes and dropped down to one knee, bracing an arm in front of her, matching him as he pushed, his eyes flashing orange. She reached out again, grabbing that orange glowing ball and squeezing, not too hard, but putting plenty of pressure on him. Mikal's face started turning red, his power flexed, attempting to dislodge her.

"Enough..." he called. Anna opened her mental grasp and retreated back into her mind. She sank down fully onto the wooden floor, gazing up at the high ceiling, panting from the exertion of using her rune casting. Mikal reached out a shaky hand and slapped the dampening bracelet back on her wrist as he too lay there, staring at the ceiling. Braun bent over, looked down into her face and sighed, reaching out to help her up. Anna ignored him, spying her chance to escape. Catching his hand and using her legs, she swept him onto the ground, using his downward momentum to help pull her up. She ran to the far end of the hall where Mikal had come in from the balcony. She thrust open the door and smacked directly into another king's guard.

"Well, we can go for a run outside through the woods if you want..." Braun remarked as he helped Mikal up. "But I am exhausted and much prefer a bath and food at the moment."

"You black hearted, evil, no good for nothing, piece of elfin offal..." she mumbled.

"Evil and black-hearted?" Braun raised a brow as he expertly maneuvered her down the hall to her suite and opened the door. The smell of lavender and lilacs brushed his nose as she stepped into the room. "Now...I would think someone of your experience could be a little more creative. I do like the black hearted though. I may have to use that during my next tirade."

Braun disappeared back down the hall to his room where he took a bath to wash off the sweat and then dressed for the day. When Juta escorted Anna to his chamber, he was wearing his breeches and a white tunic that wasn't buttoned. His feet were bare and his hair was still wet. She was escorted to the dining room and settled into the same seat as the day before. The food had been prepared while they had sparred and was ready as she eyed him carefully. He tried not to notice how her eyes worked up from the band of his breeches, across his stomach, up his chest and to his hair. He tried to ignore how aroused she had become. He couldn't afford to lose his control. Many powerful rune casters had given up using their powers and it had always ended in death for them. The power would flare out of control, the results being a spent carcass of charred ash. He wouldn't allow that to happen to himself. For the sake of his kingdom, he couldn't go down that path. He inhaled deeply. That scent of lavender and lilac floated to him across the table as she ate her food quietly. His iron clad control slipping just a little.

"There are a ton of pictures strewn across that desk in there..." she said around a mouthful of egg. "Who are they?"

"You."

"Me?" She looked up at him as if he was crazy. "Those are not me. You are serious about us knowing each other?"

"Yes, they were you twenty years ago. I admit, my skill as an artist is lacking. We do know each other, though. I promise you that we had a very deep relationship."

"And the monkey carving?"

"You remember the monkey?" His gaze flicked to the small memento he had kept from his childhood. It held a prominent spot on the bookshelves behind his desk. She swallowed a mouthful of egg, narrowed her eyes for a moment of introspection, then shrugged her shoulders.

"I remember that I had tried to carve it because my mother insisted that I have a gift for the princes on the marrow. I had just run into two boys earlier that day in the woods and had decided to carve the animals they reminded me of. I distinctly remember how much I hate wood carving. I remember giving it to you and Mikal, in your parlor room. I also remember how embarrassed I was that the two clodpolls from the forest were actually the princes of the realm." She flipped her thumb at the room behind her. Her forehead wrinkled and she slathered some butter on a biscuit before continuing. "Although the room looks different now. I also remember you two looking like popinjays ready to rescue some valiant princess and that we had run off to the stables after you two changed to play with the horses. If you call that a revival of memories...so be it."

"That's a lot to remember, but it should reinforce that I will not harm you."

"I'm still a rune caster in Enderton being held by the Corrupt King who has decreed that no rune caster shall live within his kingdom." Anna gave him a hesitant smile. "Trust that my life isn't going to be forfeit at any moment isn't going to be instantaneous Braun, simply because I remember meeting you and your brother."

"Goddess bless..." he choked out, his face going red. After a few labored breaths, he pulled his anger back under control, nodded his head, raised a brow and sipped his drink. "I see your point."

They finished the meal in silence, Anna returning to her suite so Juta could do her fittings, and he moved to his desk. A strange notion that Anna was more than she seemed floated through his mind. He knew she was Anna from twenty years ago, but there was more. Like how she knew exactly how to hold her utensils, how she knew to sit squarely at the table with her back straight, both feet planted firmly on the ground. He had watched through two meals now as she delicately picked up her linen and placed it in her lap before she began eating and then raised it to her lips, dabbing like a princess before resting it beside her trencher. These are not the skills or habits of the normal peasantry. They were quirks that she had exhibited since he had known her but were now making his mind itch with the puzzle.

How had she learned all the mannerisms of a high-born and yet was born to two peasant herbalists? Braun glanced at the map with the growing number of black markers. He pressed his fingers against the bridge of his nose and shook his head. Waiting for her to remember who she was would take forever. He didn't have much time left.

Chapter Five

"These are the colors I recommend for her, the styles, and the outfits that you should pair together..." Juta remarked as she thumbed through the book of parchment drawings. She smacked Braun's hand as another of her drawings disappeared from the stack. "Stop stealing my best work. I can't put her in that dress if you don't let me make it first.

"Perfect Juta. Whatever you find necessary." He gave her a not sorry smile and she growled, tossing her hands in the air without retrieving her missing picture. Juta moved quickly out of the study, her short stubby arms slapped her hips in exasperation.

Braun rubbed his face wearily. Anna had been here a little less than a week. They had spent every morning together training and having breakfast. They spent every evening together for the evening meal. During the time he was with her, he tried to bring her memories closer to the surface. It was obvious now that his father had employed a purple rune caster to wipe her memories. However, the purple caster his father hired was not skilled. Anna had been confronted with a few pieces of her past and memories began resurfacing. If the purple caster had been a decent one, she would not be remembering things at all. He stood from his desk, preparing to head to the dance hall for his morning training with Anna. He pulled the drawer of his desk open and dropped the drawing into it when his study door slammed open. Mikal blew in like a gust of wind, his face red with anger.

"You need to see this!" He dropped a parchment on the desk with Astrid's spidery writing on it. Braun scanned the intel quickly, dropping into his chair.

"Are you kidding me?"

"No." Mikal crossed his arms over his chest. "The Garian King has demanded that you either accept his daughter's hand in marriage or you forfeit the mountains. What are you planning to do?"

"What can I do?" Ben stood from the desk and began pacing back and forth. "I have a powerful solution to my problem just down the hall from this room right now...but she is still remembering who she is, what her powers are, and how to use them! Meanwhile, I have the Garian's demanding I make their daughter my consort."

"Queen..." Mikal corrected with a derisive snort. Braun only glared at him.

"Consort. Those imposters are not royalty. Which is the right answer for the kingdom?" He turned his face to Mikal and let his exhaustion out in a slow breath. "Which one brother? Tell me, for I am at a loss."

"You are the King, Ben." Mikal gave him a smile and a wink. "I am sure you will have an answer to benefit all of our people. Sleep on it. Your dreams will show you the answer." He frowned when his brother groaned. "What?"

"That is the problem...my dreams...Anna" Ben almost stabbed something in frustration. "I need to get out of here. Mikal, I need you to take over her training for a few days."

"Ben..." he started. The look of desperation that crossed his brothers face made him stop. "Alright. Is it that bad?"

"With Anna...it always has been." Ben ran his hands through his hair and groaned. "Her smell, her voice, even just the whisper of her name and I am on edge. She amplifies my power ten-fold. This is why my power surged twenty years ago when mother and father took her away. The thought of never being near her again..." Ben tugged on his hair in frustration.

"You are that in love with her?" Mikal shook his head in awe. "She is a commoner."

Ben shrugged and raised a brow. "Do I really have a choice in the matter? My white runes call to her black runes as if we were made for each other. My heart beats in time with hers. And I know," Ben held his hands up in surrender. "I can't sound any more besotted than I already am, but that woman is under my skin. Damnation, she is my skin, as raw and exposed as it feels right now. I need time away. I need time to release some power."

"Go. I'll handle her training. The last thing we need is you to flare up again, making that worse..." he growled, motioning to the hand carved map against the far side of the room.

Ben clapped his brother on the back and strode into his chamber. He filled a pack with a few changes of clothes and then headed down to the courtyard. By the time he got there, Mikal had another pack with food and a few weapons. He climbed astride his black horse and took off without much thought. He knew his brother would keep everything together. He knew that while he was taking care of his power flare, Mikal would be taking care of Anna. Jealousy burned for a moment in his gut as he thought about his brother training with Anna. The thought was almost unbearable. He was seconds away from turning his mount around and heading back. The trouble with his kingdom happened for this very same reason. He needed to keep moving until he could safely release his rune power.

• • • •

"GOOD MORNING, ANNA..." Mikal said with a dip of his head. Anna paused halfway to the middle of the dance floor, her eyes scanned him from head to toe and then glanced around the room. "Ah, King Braun had to leave for a while. He has requested that I continue your training. During that time, you may take your meals in your room or join the men in the mess hall."

"How long will he be gone?"

"What?" Mikal asked, falling into a ready stance just as she had. He watched as she followed his slow methodical movements.

"How long did you say he would be gone?"

"A few days maybe..." he felt her telepathy as it brushed the surface of his mind. He wondered if she realized she had access to her power again. The bracelet was obviously worn out. It had only lasted a week. Mikal shook his head in awe, switching the movements to a left-handed stance. Anna was damned powerful. A normal rune caster wearing a bracelet would have it on for almost two months before it wore out. In one week, she had zapped the dampening strength of the bracelet. "It is hard to say...one with his type of power...well...you can imagine how they have to be released every now and then." Mikal watched as jealously, anger, and rage galloped across her face, but then settled once more into the serene mask of indifference. She didn't like the thought of Ben having relations with another woman. Very interesting. The mutual attraction brought a smile to his face.

"One would think," she huffed out as she turned and began running. She didn't wait for him to join her. "Being the King of Enderton, that he would have plenty of doxies lined up in a room somewhere here inside his castle." She darted her gaze over to Mikal and watched as he just grinned from ear to ear and shrugged his shoulders. "Oh...but maybe he has a taste for the more unusual..."

"Naw, he likes women, not men." Mikal stopped her mid jog and took a swing. She countered easily enough. He pushed a little more aggressively than Braun did and watched as she skillfully pressed back her advantage. "I have been watching my brothers' sessions with you...he hasn't taught you these moves...where did you learn them?"

"I know a lot of things I refuse to tell you. Doesn't mean that asking about them will get you the answer." Her eyes lit up as she made a plan. They went through the whole morning training routine before Mikal escorted her back to her suite.

"Mikal..." Anna asked, biting her lower lip. She watched as he leaned against the wall next to her room. She placed one hand on the door knob, then leaned closer to him. She watched as his gaze fastened on her lips. "Do you think maybe I could go for a ride? It is awfully stuffy inside this castle and I haven't had any fresh air for a very long time."

"Not in this lifetime, sweet lips." Mikal chuckled, slapped her on the backside, then ambled down the hall. "And I definitely wouldn't tell my brother you just tried to use your guile when you wanted something."

"You are a worthless piece of elfin guts, you dwarven..." her curses rang through the hall as she stepped into her room. She must have been taking notes from Juta as those curses were getting pretty shrewd. Mikal's laughter rang down the hall as he headed off to his rooms. Anna cringed at the sound of his laughter. Memories of someone laughing in a similar way floated just out of her reach. She remembered them as brothers and having met them, but that was all. Juta assisted her to the tub and pulled out her gown for the day.

Once her anger simmered down slightly, Anna thought about her situation. She had a few days to plan an escape. She could sneak out through the windows of this room. She had noticed that there were hardly any guards that patrolled the castle walls. She would run across the battlements, drop down at the clump of trees that came extremely close and take off into the woods. Four days and she would be back in Garia. All she needed was a few items she could pilfer easily enough. Juta seemed to keep an ever-watchful eye on her, but Anna knew she would be able to sneak past her.

Chapter Six

"She ran, your highness..." Astrid grumbled in shame as Ben reigned his horse up into the courtyard four days later.

"Curse Mikal and Juta." Ben turned his horse, forgetting that he was exhausted and needed rest. "Where in the kingdom is he?"

"He went to retrieve her. A few of our trackers last reported signs of her near Amberside, here..." Astrid pointed on a map to the last area they had seen her. She watched as the King headed east.

Ben couldn't believe this. How could Mikal and Juta have let her escape? He had hoped that his own brother would be strong enough to keep one woman under lock and key for a few days. Now he rode like a mad man to catch up to them. He couldn't let her disappear again. His heart couldn't handle it.

• • • •

ANNA KNELT QUIETLY in the tree. Her brown breeches and green shirt were enough to help her blend in so that none of the men below had glimpsed her once. She groaned softly when Braun rode into the woods. The dark circles under his eyes were so pronounced, she could see them from ten feet up in the tree. He was wearing a pair of tan leather breeches, and a cream-colored tunic that laced up his chest. He looked very handsome but worn out. She reached out with her power and prodded his power gently. He was still overloaded. He hadn't expelled any power while he had been away. Part of her was elated to find out he hadn't slept with a woman. The other part of her was fearful. He was playing with fire if he didn't do something soon.

Frowning, she dipped her gaze, watching as he turned and looked up in her direction. She held her breath as his eyes locked onto hers. He opened his mouth, his arm raised slightly, and then his eyes closed and he dropped from the horse. Anna felt her heart beat quicken. Braun began to glow very faintly. Cursing, she slipped down a few branches. His men and brother would know what was happening. She would wait to make sure he was taken care of and then she would continue to Garia.

"What happened?" Mikal demanded of the few men standing around. All of them shook their heads, raised their shoulders, or stood there with their mouths open catching flies. "Ben!" he slapped him on the face, expecting a reaction.

"Jyake, get a tent set up. We can't leave until we get the King back on his feet."

"Will he be alright?" an unfamiliar soldier asked. Mikal assessed him for a moment.

"He will be fine..." he assured the man. Once he was out of earshot, he mumbled to himself. "Once I figure out what is wrong with him."

Anna sighed, dropping her shoulders and rolling her eyes. She may not have the highest education on rune casting, but she at least knew what a power flare looked like. She glanced to the east and felt her body's yearning to be home. Then she glanced down at the two men she had known as boys. Like a flash rainstorm in the spring, her memories of everything returned. She remembered meeting the boys in the forest as a child. She could recount the day they had been introduced formally through her parents and his. She could even remember the night that Ben had cornered her in these very woods, trying to do exactly what he needed to do now. She could even remember how their father had carved the lovely scar into her face. The feelings she had for the two men below simmered under her skin. She glanced once more towards Garia. She would have to return home at another time. She couldn't leave the man she was in love with dying on the forest floor. Anna growled like an angry cat as she dropped out of the trees. Mikal's head whipped around in her direction, his hand on a dagger at his belt.

"Anna!" he said in a strangled voice as he motioned his men to back away from her. She dropped to her knees next to them.

"Relax Mikal." Anna gave him a fond smile, patting his arm. She turned her full attention to Ben. Her hand dropped to his forehead and she frowned as Mikal caught her wrist. "What..." she stammered.

"You know what this is?" he asked, removing the bracelet from her wrist with a sad smile. He watched as she nodded but then began undressing his brother, starting at his feet.

"He hasn't released his power Mikal...reach out and see for yourself."

"What...he..." Mikal did as she prompted and expelled several heated curses. "The bloody idiot. He left so he could. What was he thinking?"

Anna shrugged, tugging his boots off. "My guess is he got side-tracked. Whatever the reason his powering is flaring. He is running a fever and we need to get that down as fast as possible or he may succumb and burn up."

"What..." Mikal swallowed, balling his hands into fists. "Whatever you need Anna. We are yours to command."

"Feverfew. I need a bundle about this big..." she held her hands out. "It needs to be boiled and then simmered into a tea. We will have to pour it down his throat. Cold water from the river, lots of it. Two buckets for now to start. I need him put into the tent on a cot. As many blankets as you can spare."

Anna watched as Mikal began commanding the men. Two of them put him inside the tent where Anna finished stripping off his leather breeches and his tunic. She thanked the men who dropped blankets down next to her and the other man who brought her two buckets of water from the stream. Breaking the fever would be the easiest part of the problem. The hard part would be containing his power. Her mind toyed with the options. She could give herself bodily to the man she loved and his power flare would disappear. It would be the easiest course of action. Could she bring herself to do that though? She had never been with a man physically and while she knew now that she loved him, was she ready to take that step. Did he love her? She knew she couldn't give herself physically to a man unless he loved her in return. What was she thinking? He was a KING. He couldn't love someone as common as she was. Inhaling deeply, she began washing his body with cold water and a cloth. Why couldn't his rune blasted power be something other than white?

"Anna..." Mikal said, ducking into the tent. He dropped down onto his knees next to her, grabbing a cloth and bathing his brother beside her. "You plan to run again?"

"No..." The constricted sound of her voice made him raise a brow at her. "I couldn't imagine it now."

"You finally remember everything?"

"Yes..." she exhaled. Anna swiped a tear from her eye and dipped her cloth into the cold water. She lightly brushed the cloth down Ben's chest and his arm snapped out, reflexively knocking her back. "Even with a fever he is strong...he will make it through this."

"When did your memories come back?" Mikal watched her closely, like a hawk circling its prey.

"A few moments ago. When he dropped from his horse, I knew I had my chance to run, to get home, but then I looked at you kneeling over him with worry in your eyes and something inside clicked into place. I couldn't leave...not like this. Especially not with everything that I have finally figured out."

"What have you figured out?"

"All of this..." she motioned toward the forest and beyond. "The fact that he 'hates' rune casters and executes them is a lie. He is playing a long game with the Mawhorter's." Anna dropped her gaze and sighed with exhaustion. "I have hated Astrid, you, and him for years because I thought you were killing off our people. Now I know that Ben would never be able to kill a rune caster in cold blood. I hated you and Astrid because I thought you were doing his dirty work. I now know and remember neither of you could be that cold hearted either."

"You love him." It didn't seem like a question. Mikal made it a simple statement of fact. When her hands hesitated, he broke out that lopsided jovial grin. "It is not a big deal. I've known since we were kids that you two were meant for each other. Anyone with eyes could have seen that. Even our obtuse father could see that."

"I'm no good for him." She inhaled a shaky breath, her mental power prodding Ben's. It flared, growing bigger. "He needs a princess or a royal or even just a Goddess blessed power match. He doesn't need a common peasant woman who knows nothing but how to sneak around and make herbal medicines."

"Gaia only know what he needs...and she wouldn't put two together unless it had some sense to it." Mikal caught her arm and motioned outside the tent. "It's going to be a long afternoon and night. I suggest we take this in turns. You go make the tea. Jyake should be back with a bundle of feverfew now. I'll continue to bath him and then we can switch off for rest breaks."

Anna couldn't argue with his logic. She crawled out of the tent, suddenly feeling every single one of her thirty-eight years. Her body pained her as she stood and stretched. She was going soft. A little over a week sleeping on a soft moss filled mattress and then three days sleeping on the hard ground and she was acting like she was a hundred years old. Jyake indeed had returned with a nice bundle of feverfew. She stripped the herbs, dropped them into a pot of water sitting it over the campfire and stirred them around as she waited for it to boil.

Gaia would only put two together if it made sense. She snorted to herself as she stirred. Those were pretty words from Mikal. She only wished that it was the truth. Her heart ached with the need to be loved. She wanted to confess her love, be wrapped up into those strong arms, and rest her head on his shoulder. She wanted him to kiss her thoroughly, his strong fingers wrapping up in her hair, pressing against her with need. She felt the familiar singing in her veins as her cheeks warmed with those thoughts. Rune points! Ben's power was slipping even more. She moved the pot off the fire and to the side as the water began to boil.

Mentally, Anna poked his power again, watching as it grew once more. What could she do? The only way a rune caster could release their power was to use it. That meant he needed to unleash his unbridled passion, but she wasn't going to volunteer for that, at least not yet. She could try siphoning his powers and funneling them into the earth. She looked around at the forest of Border Town. It was full of ancient oaks, maples and cherry trees. There were blackberry and mulberry bushes that popped up in the few random places the tree foliage was thin.

As the sun dipped lower in the sky, the birds and squirrels slowed their chirping and chattering. The crickets and frogs began to make their chorus. She heard the soft gurgle of the river not far away. Even the sounds of the camp around her were calming. The ten men with Mikal had arranged the largest tent in the middle near the camp fire. The rest were in a circle around them. The sounds of the horses rustling in a make-shift pen made her long to ride them freely through the woods towards home. She poured the finished tea into a water flask and moved back into the tent.

"You'll have to hold him, I'm not strong enough..." Anna held the water flask to Ben's mouth, hoping he would automatically take the drink. When he didn't, Mikal tilted his head back and pried his mouth open. They were able to force some liquid down his throat. "I'll take over. Go get your evening meal and a rest."

"I can have one of the men..."

"No." She waved him off, finding a fresh bucket of cold water. "I've got this. Call it my penance for running off."

"Oh, you'll have a penance for that...just not this." Mikal chuckled, ducking out of the tent. "Ben can be very imaginative in that respect."

Anna spent most of the evening and the first half of the night bathing Ben in cold water. Her imagination was working overtime as her hands skimmed over his toned body. He had long powerful legs, a trim waist, and strong arms. He lashed out several times, knocking her down. She was going to have several bruises when he was done. Her hands absently trailed over the two small parallel scars on his left shoulder. They were old and almost silver with age. She wondered how he got those. Then her hand trailed over to the pink ugly puckered scar on over his right hip. That one had to have hurt. She ran her finger across the angry slash, imaging what type of fight he had obtained it from. She felt his power expand and cursed herself for an idiot. She couldn't touch him or she would make the situation worse. Mikal appeared with Jyake. They thrust a bowl of porridge into her hands and then fought to get the tea she had brewed into Ben. When they were successful in getting some of it down his throat, Anna returned to bathing him.

She definitely wasn't well schooled in rune casting. In fact, her parents were both ordinary, so she still wasn't sure how she had gotten lucky enough to have powers. With ordinary parents though, she hadn't been trained in much but the common knowledge. Rune casters had mental and physical powers. Some were stronger in one than the other. If you didn't use the powers occasionally, you could flare out and either cause extreme damage to the land and people around you or you would burn up into a crispy charred pile of flesh. The only other thing her parents could tell her was that using her powers to force people into doing things against their will was wrong. That was all she had learned from them. The rest she had just figured out herself. She brushed a stray lock of wet black hair off Ben's forehead and let out a wistful sigh.

Ben was far from the Corrupt King everyone had claimed he was. He had not forced any woman to succumb to his power while she had known him. She knew from stories told around fires at night that there had only been one other white rune caster in history. That man had used his mental ability to push men and women alike to do what he wanted. He forced them to bend to his will, wanting only the pleasure he could wring from them. This had led the continent to split into two factions. One side for the 'Corrupt King' and one against. That was how Garia and Enderton had formed. Garia was against the 'Corrupt King' and had held the border between them by sheer force for several years. They had kept the King so overrun with fighting and skirmishes that he was unable to use his power. He was found one morning in a tent on the border, burned and charred to death. His throne to Enderton was passed down to one of his illegitimate children and thus was how Ben's parents had come to rule. It was a relief to see that he wasn't going down the path of his forefather.

A fresh bucket of cold water was brought to her at some point and she thanked the person fleetingly as she switched cloths and buckets. She reached out with her black rune power and wrapped Ben's white rune power up in hers. She had done something similar with Mikal earlier in the week when they had been training. With Mikal, she had wrapped her power around his like a blanket and squeezed, watching as he almost passed out from lack of air. Now, with Ben, she used her power like a fine netting to help hold his power in. She tucked and folded her powers around his, gritting her teeth as his passion flared at the contact. The tighter she wrapped his power up, the more chance she would have to contain it. Her hands continued to bath his body as her mind worked. When she was confident that he wouldn't be able to escape her grasp, she began to siphon off the excessive amount of power. She funneled it down through her body and out into the ground she was kneeling on. Mikal eventually stepped into the tent, rubbing his blurry eyes and yawning. He saw her black eyes, the dark shadows around her, the faint glow of runes as they scattered about the ground and he panicked.

"NO!" he shouted, grabbing her by the shoulders and shaking her out of her trance. "You can't siphon his power into the earth."

"But..." she started, her mind having trouble focusing. She struggled against Mikal's strong grip as she gazed down at Ben. His fever seemed to be breaking and he was covered in sweat. "It's working."

"But you are killing the land!" he accused, pointing down at the ground. Her gaze followed his hand and she slumped.

"I had no idea..."

"Just don't push any more into the earth. Gaia doesn't like it..." Mikal ran his fingers through his hair and dropped down next to her. "Go get some rest. I'll take over from here."

Chapter Seven

It took two days to completely rid Ben of the fever and for him to regain enough of his strength to stay in his saddle. Anna felt it was a good idea to stay out of his tent while he was awake. There was no sense in antagonizing the man and making his power grow even more. As it was, her powers were still wrapped around his and she found herself taking several cold baths in the river at night. Knowing how much she loved him and how much she wanted to be with him made their powers touching even harder to bear. She looked sadly at the area around the tent where she had pushed his powers. The grass was starting to turn brown and shrivel up. The trees were starting to wilt, the leaves dropping to the ground, half brown and half green. The shrubs lost all their berries overnight, the limbs falling to the ground. This must be what they needed her to help fix, but how could she? She had funneled his power from him and to the ground and still it had caused this. She reflexively accepted a bowl of food from a guard that walked past her. Her body seemed to work on automatic more in the last few days than it ever had. She took a few bites and then sat the bowl down next to her. Someone gave the order to break camp and set out for the castle. Her gaze focused one last time on the east. She had been so close to home.

There was very little for her to do as the men had pretty much broken down the camp that night. They were tying up the last of the tents and collecting sleeping bags. She was standing in the middle of the camp, wringing her hands, feeling filthy even though she had taken several dips in the river. Her mind was focused so tightly on what she had done to the forest and how she could fix it, she barely recognized being picked up. It wasn't until she was settled down against a pair of rock-hard thighs and a solid muscular chest that her mind snapped back to the present. Ben's arms wrapped around her waist and grabbed the reins of his horse. He still had deep purple smudges beneath his beautiful brown eyes. He had taken a dip this morning in the river and smelled like the water, the earth, and his own spicy scent. She inhaled deeply, reacting and snuggling back against his body. She heard him groan deep in his throat and she sat up, her power flexing slightly as his grew. His arms wrapped around her and tugged her back and she relented. It was either ride in his lap or she had to walk. As tired as she was, she didn't care at the moment.

"Thank you..." he murmured against her ear. She could feel the rasp of his beard against the curve of her ear and she suppressed a shiver. "And your punishment will be forthcoming."

"I'm sure it will..." She ground her teeth and looked behind them at the damage she had caused. "But no need to thank me. I think I just made your original problem worse..."

"No, you didn't..." he chuckled deep in his throat and rested a hand against her thigh. "If you had, that would be black and dead by now. In fact, that is hardly the start of it. Gaia does seem to hate my power. I'm not sure how the white craft came to be, but it probably didn't originate with Gaia."

"Nonsense. I may not be smart in this, but all of the craft came from Gaia. It is with her consecration that we are blessed to expand her powers to heal her land and brighten her skies."

"What?" Ben turned her face so he could look into her eyes. "Where did you get that from?"

"It...um...well..." Anna shifted with nerves. "I learned it from a friend."

"Well, that is the first I have heard it explained that way."

Ben settled her back against his chest, inhaling her intoxicating scent of lilacs and lavender. He could still feel his power flaring, but he also felt her power. He had studied rune craft since he was a child and first started showing signs. He had never been taught or had seen in a book that rune craft could be used to contain another. He thought it was pretty clever. He would never have thought to do it. Of course, he knew, deep down, it wasn't a solution to his problem. He needed to alleviate his power naturally, but he couldn't.

He had disappeared for those few days to find some random woman in a village to tussle with. He had found plenty of them. He had spent a whole day in a tavern, drinking plenty of ale, working up the commitment to taking one of them to bed. It wasn't until he was so drunk, he could barely walk that he stopped fighting his inner conscious. He was in love with Anna. He couldn't roll around in the sheets with any other woman. It had to be her. He had grabbed his horse and headed back to the castle when he had found out that she had run.

They spent three torturous days in the saddle, taking a few extra breaks through the days as he was still regaining his strength. When they finally rode into the castle proper, Ben found himself at a loss as to what his next steps should be. He had half a continent that needed to be healed, a Garian royal decree that demanded an answer, and his power flaring out of control. What was the first step to take? He caught Anna's well-rounded hips in his hands and set her down on the ground. She nodded her head in thanks, turning her back to him and quickly moving into the castle. A stable boy took the reins of his horse and he followed Anna, trying hard not to step into her room when she did.

He knew which of the pressing issues he wanted to resolve, but he couldn't. He couldn't force her. Making his way to his chambers, he found a very hot and relaxing bath had already been drawn, and he sank into it gratefully. While he had taken a dip in the river, it was nothing compared to scrubbing off the dirt and sweat from a week in the saddle. He pulled on his black breeches and a pale blue laced up tunic, leaving his boots in his room. He didn't plan on going anywhere today. He had travelled enough for a little while. He was just moving through a stack of missives that had arrived while he was gone when he heard a knock on the door.

"Ben?" Mikal called. He opened the door to the study a crack. His brother was reading a missive, the wrinkle on his forehead growing bigger by the second. "Ah...I see you are getting the news then."

"They can't be serious..." Ben pressed his fingers against the bridge of his nose. "The Garian's are very persistent. If only we could get the Mawhorter's off that throne..."

"I'm afraid they are serious." Mikal dropped into the chair across from him and propped one foot on top of the other. "I heard it from a chamber maid coming out of my rooms. It appears someone has been snooping around in your office. I'll have Astrid look into it immediately."

"There is no end to this...is there?"

"Not for the King..."

"Let me see if I have this right." Ben leaned his head back against the chair and steepled his fingers. "I am in the middle of a potentially earth-shattering power flare that is only being held at bay by the woman who is causing it to flare." He ground his teeth together and dropped his hands to the arms of the chair. "I, the King of Enderton, am being commanded by a foreign delegation to answer their demands to marry their daughter or forfeit my rights to the dwarven mountains in the north. On top of all of that, there is a rune casted blight that I produced that is killing off all vegetation on my side of the continent that is slowly starving my people and with that, there are only two solutions. I either marry the princess and my people will then have free access to the Garian food stores or I somehow convince Anna that she is a black rune caster and we miraculously concoct a solution to my previous egregious error."

"Yeah...that sounds about right." Mikal slapped his knee and smiled brightly. "But on the bright side, Anna is back."

Ben only shook his head, dropped his shoulders, and sighed.

"Your highness..." a strong female voice murmured after tapping on the door.

"Come in Juta." Ben turned to face her as she entered.

"I heard some of the servants talking about a possible ball..."

"Yes..."

"I thought you might want me to create some gowns for Anna. Something more appropriate than the simple ones..."

"Excellent idea..."

"I'll just leave this stack here for you to peruse at your leisure and don't steal any of the sketches, your highness." Juta swept out of the room, her blonde ponytail swishing with her movements.

"Now we have a ball we have to prepare for...with less than perfect food..."

"You know, all of this would be solved if we could find the lost Garian princess." Mikal stood, his gaze roaming over the books on the wall. "Where did you put father's books from his investigation?"

"Over there..." Ben motioned to the side of the room where the dagger was stabbed into the shelf. "Why?"

"There is something that has been tickling my mind for a while. I think there is something missing."

Mikal filched the book off the shelf and strode towards the door. It wasn't until the door to his study closed with a click that Ben realized he was alone. He had been studying the sketches that Juta had made for Anna. Juta was a very talented artist and the designs she came up with only enhanced Anna's beauty. They were so vivid and lifelike. He swallowed hard, itching to steal the whole book. He selected two gowns and moved the stack reverently to the edge of his desk. The rest of his afternoon was spent going through ledgers and missives. His eyes kept straying back to Juta's drawing as he thought about the missing Garian princess.

When he was five, he had been engaged to the three-year-old Garian princess. They had met once as their parents signed the agreements or did whatever they did to make it official. He didn't remember much about it. Who could remember their childhood? Two years after that agreement had been made, the kingdom of Garia had experienced a large upheaval. The King and Queen were murdered by rioters. The princess had either been kidnapped, killed, or was well hidden. The kingdom was in chaos as the man who had murdered Aylex and Lily seated himself on the throne. He claimed that he was the true heir. King and Queen Mawhorter had been running their country into the ground, taxing their people so highly they could barely afford to eat. A month ago, Ben had toyed with the idea of marrying Princess Elena. It would allow him the ability to feed his people and give him the opportunity to rid Garia of the greed and taxes. His eyes strayed back to the hand drawing of Anna.

Goddess why couldn't she be the missing Garian princess? He would rally his troops behind her. He would ride down every dissenter in her kingdom and seat her back on the throne. He would then bend his knee and swear his allegiance and his half of the continent to her. Ben thought of all the odd ball quirks that Anna exhibited. As a child they had teased her for not remembering much of her childhood. Ben remembered asking her if she had ridden a horse much as a child. She had gone statue still, her eyes took on a faraway look, and then she shrugged her shoulders and pulled herself expertly into the saddle of the pony. Peasants didn't usually ride horses much, and when they did, it was usually bareback as they couldn't afford saddles.

She had done other things as well. For her fifteenth birthday, his parents had hosted a dinner party at the castle. He had expected her to fumble with the proper etiquette. It came as a shock when she sat straighter than the other ladies. She had eaten like a lady, talked about appropriate topics ladies would talk about, and even danced a waltz with grace. He had to believe there was more to her than he knew. His door opened without a knock and Juta strode inside.

"I have made the decision. I will be hosting a festival in two weeks to announce my engagement and to welcome the Garian delegation." Ben remarked with determination. "I want these two gowns made for Anna. I want the first one to be purple, white and black. I'll leave the rest up to you." He held the sketched out as Juta reached for them. "When you are done using this, I want the drawings for myself."

"Along with the other half dozen you have sticky fingered into your drawer..." Juta nodded her head as other servants and house members entered. Ben only grinned boyishly at Juta and nodded his head. He gave the other servants instructions on preparations for the ball. The flurry of activity must have reached his brothers room, for he finally returned to the study a few hours later.

"You've made up your mind I hear?" Mikal inquired.

"Yes." Ben let out a sigh. "I have decided."

"If you do what I am sure you are going to do, you can't keep up the charade that you are the Corrupt King."

"It was getting a little monotonous anyway. We have been playing the long game too long." Ben turned pleading eyes to Mikal as his door opened and Anna was thrust inside by a pair of small dwarven hands. She looked exhausted but more refreshed than she had on the way back to the castle. He motioned her to the dining room, not realizing the day was already gone. "My options are limited."

"Then we shall face it together, brother." Mikal smiled, crossing his arms over his chest as his brother's whole attention focused on the woman seated at his private table. "I found something in one of our father's notes..."

"And?" Ben asked casually, not giving him much attention as he gravitated towards Anna. "We have been through those things a million times."

"I need to go check it out. I shall return before the festival and your announcement..."

"Wait...what?" Ben demanded, turning just as his brother left. Grumbling, he settled in for dinner, enjoying the deep red of her dress against her creamy white skin. Anna kept her head down. She hardly looked at him through the meal. When she did look up, she made sure to focus on his left ear. Her answers to his questions were simple and to the point. Gone was the snarky sass he had been getting used to. "Anna, are you going to run away again?"

"No," she sighed, dipping her gaze back to her trencher.

"Why am I so fortunate?" Ben eased back in his chair, almost afraid of what she was going to say. Fear clenched his gut as he waited. The way his luck was running, he could only imagine what she was going to say. "You were perfectly capable of eluding my guards, Mikal, and Juta."

"I..." her lip trembled and a tear slipped out of the corner of her eye. She focused once again on her trencher, using her spoon to push food around. "I...just can't...won't."

"Anna, please look at me." Her gaze focused on his left ear. "Thank you for helping me hold my power in. Without you I would be damaging the kingdom more than I have already, but that can't be the only reason you are refusing to run again."

"I have found my heart is here," she whispered.

"What was that?" He was dumbfounded. His hearing must be impaired.

She cleared her throat and turned her gaze directly into his, her hands trembling as she sat her spoon down. "My heart is here, in this castle. I can't and won't run, for if I did, it would surely kill me."

"Your heart is..." he raised a brow and scrubbed at his face in pure undisguised frustration and anger. Nothing was ever going to be easy. "Whom have you fallen in love with Anna?"

She shook her head, holding eye contact even as he felt his heart break.

"Who is it? I won't be angry, just help me understand. I have made very meticulous plans to keep you with a rotating guard. There is no way you could have fallen in love with any of them in a day."

She shrugged, biting her pouty bottom lip. The pulse of his magic flared at that movement and her breath caught in her throat.

Her power tamped down his passion as his anger and jealousy blazed hotter.

"Anna, I have to ask who..."

"I will do it."

"Do what?" Ben couldn't keep half this conversation straight. He watched as she rose from her chair.

"I will use my power to heal your kingdom. I will help ease your power flare. I will do whatever you command, Your Highness."

Hope ignited in his gut for the briefest of moments as he watched her lowered gaze. She had called him your highness instead of Braun. He wasn't sure if he was thrilled with that idea or not. It meant she was finally coming to see him as a person instead of the Corrupt King, as the boy she had known. Yet, he missed her saucy contemptible way of spitting his last name out, almost as if it was a pet name. He liked how she pushed against his orders and demands. He loved her fiery passion. Rune points, he had even respected her for escaping the confines of his guards and castle. It would have been unseemly if she hadn't tried at least once to escape. He watched as she took her leave, her hair sweeping her shoulders as she walked, the shorter Garian styled skirt giving him a perfect view of her calves. Ben waved one of the servants to clean up the remains of dinner. Blast it all. He was exhausted and just wanted to sleep. He needed time. He needed to be free of all of this. Not for the first time, he cursed his mother and father, yet again, for leaving him this kingdom.

Chapter Eight

B en stood over Anna as she slept. He had tried sleeping, but he couldn't. Every time he closed his eyes, he dreamed of her. The moonlight streamed through the window, casting her in a pale silhouette against the black sheets of her bed. The flimsy black silk that Juta dressed her in did nothing to hide her luscious curves from his view. His fingers itched to comb through her soft mahogany curls as they lay scattered about her pillow. Anna moaned softly and thrashed around on the bed, her body gravitating closer to him. He reacted physically to her. His need swelling to almost bursting as he watched her rosy pink lips open and close. She was breathing heavily as her eyes fluttered and snapped open. She didn't shout or scream at the sight of him staring down at her. Ben wondered if she was frightened at all. Her cheeks looked flushed in her pale creamy skin, beads of sweat dotted her brow, and her chest rose and fell quickly.

He dropped to his knees next to the bed, holding her doe eyed gaze, praying to Gaia that his White Rune craft would just disappear. He was tired of wanting her. Closing his eyes, he tilted his head back and breathed a quick prayer. Ben fell back on his bum when Anna's fingers whispered against his shoulder. His eyes shot open to find her leaning out of the bed, a worried look crossing her face as she brushed her lips against his forehead. He knew she was checking him for a fever. Her power was tightening around his. She was making sure he wasn't flaring out of control. He reached up, capturing her hips in his hands, and pulled her out of the bed and into his lap. She gasped in surprise but didn't cry out in alarm.

"Anna..." he whispered against her forehead. His lips caressed the soft curve of her neck. She tasted like sweat and honey. She turned, pressing her chest against him as she wrapped her fingers through his hair. "I can't hold on..."

"It's okay..." she whispered as she gave him a quick peck on the cheek. "You don't have to hold on anymore. I have you..."

Ben groaned, capturing her lips with a hunger he had never felt before. She mewled softly like a kitten as her hands ran up and down his back, along his shoulders and chest, back to his hair. She was creating a trail of fire everywhere she touched. Growling, he broke the kiss and peppered her face and neck with nips and kisses, working down to the deep dip of her gown. The fabric strained against her breasts. He cupped one in his free hand, looking up as Anna sighed her silky hair spilling across his arm. She arched her back as he flicked his nail against her nipple. The soft groan from her throat had him grasping the top of her gown and ripping it open without thought. He captured her nipple in his mouth, lavishing his tongue around it in circles. Her fingers were clasped in his hair again, her back arching more. He felt her fingers glide across his bare chest, running light circles around his nipples. His groin tightened even more in response. He tipped his head back, as her lips trailed down his neck and throat. Ben groaned when her tongue dipped into the hollow at the base of his throat. He wrapped his arms around her, stood, and eased her softly onto the bed. The pool of silk laying forgotten on the floor.

From the full glow of the moon behind him, Ben drank in the sight of her. The tiny ankles, the long legs and thighs, the dark apex of her womanhood to the swell of her hips, the nip of her waist, up to the roundness of her breasts and to her long neck. She was all his. He couldn't deny himself any longer. He needed her like he needed oxygen. His gaze caught hers, flashing white hot, and he felt something stir inside of him. She was looking at him with such trust, it almost broke him. Spreading her legs, he kneeled down, placing her feet on his shoulder. Anna gasped, coming off the bed the moment his tongue grazed her hidden recess. He pressed her back against the bed with one hand, continuing his onslaught. He felt her body clench tight against his fingers. She was so sweet and salty he reminded himself to go slowly or he would burst from his need. He felt her body tremble, then shake, and her gasp of pleasure as she crested her wave of passion. Smiling, he kissed his way up her body, capturing her lips for another kiss. He looked down into her eyes, seeing her pupils dilated. His power had escaped his control. She was under his white caster power influence.

"Braun...I..." she pleaded. Her hands scrambled around, making him cry out with need as she brushed against his breeches. She stilled, those eyes looking up at him in confusion. "Did I hurt you?"

"You..." he swallowed and did an inner reflection. Her power was still wrapped tightly around his. His power hadn't leaked. Her dilated eyes were not from his rune craft. He almost crumpled at the realization that she truly wanted him. "You can't hurt me...not like this...not ever"

"Braun..." she whimpered, her hands fumbling against his breeches.

"Ben..." Ben begged her softly. He caught her hands in his, removing the offending cloth so he was naked next to her. Her eyes took him in much the same as he had done before. She hesitantly reached down and wrapped those tiny but warm fingers around his member. He bucked against her as she began a rhythm that had him panting in moments. Catching her hand, he pressed her back into the soft mattress. Her legs instinctively parted as he settled between her thighs. Her body cradled his perfectly. It was as if they were meant to be together.

"Ben..." she finally pleaded, her hands grasping frantically at his shoulders. With a quick push, he was inside her. Her flinch almost escaped his attention. He wanted to buck and press like a wild stallion as his need grew stronger inside her tight body. Holding himself as still as he could, he waited for her body to readjust. When she began panting and bucking against him, he lost all control. Ben thrust into her over and over again as her body began to tighten like a spring around him. When she reached her crest, her back arched, her pelvis thrust against his, and she called his name once again. He pressed into her one last time, letting go of his control as he spilled himself inside of her warm welcome honey pot. Ben could have sworn the heavens were sighing as he lay on his side, panting and covered in sweat. Anna still had her hips locked around his, her head lay back against his arm, her breath tickling his throat. He didn't want to move, he couldn't. This was where he should be forever.

"Anna..." he murmured softly, pulling her even closer.

"Ben..." she whispered back.

"Thank you...for the release." He brushed her hair with his hands, running those silky strands through his fingers. "You didn't have to..."

"I know." Anna grabbed his ears in her hands and tilted his face down to look into hers. She was still panting, the chill of the evening air after their exercise causing goosebumps to rise along her arms. "Your power has drained..." she mumbled against his lips as she kissed him.

"It..." he chuckled as her mouth trailed kisses along his neck, his chin, across his shoulder. "It has, yes. I should leave you to get some rest...I know we are both bone-weary."

"Ben...if you leave this bed," her teeth sunk teasingly into his shoulder. "I will geld you. I told you no a long time ago and I regret that now. Show me more."

"As you command..." he conceded.

Chapter Nine

"Anna..." Juta called as she stepped through the door. "Oh Gaia...beg your pardon, Your Highness!" Juta exclaimed, as she shut the door quickly. Anna snorted and tucked her head back under Ben's chin, blocking the sun as it slowly peeked over the horizon and through the window. Ben had tried to get out of bed at least two hours ago, but Anna kept pulling him back and wrapping her arms and legs around him. She checked his power mentally. He was hardly pulsing with power right now. He could handle it on his own from here. She removed her black power net from around white orb.

"Anna..." Ben whispered against the top of her hair. "I may be a King, but I can't lie abed all day."

"Why not?" She nipped his collarbone and felt his member stiffen against her thigh. She rolled her eyes as Ben tried to climb out of bed yet again. "You have had a very stressful time lately. As the source for your very recent release, I think you need more time to rest." He pulled himself into a sitting position, the sheet tucked around his waist as he grabbed his breeches off the floor.

"I have a kingdom to run...and you..." he pinned her against the bed after pulling his breeches on. A deep breath escaped as those bright brown eyes looked straight into his soul. "You, my wicked darling, have to be fit for a gown." He watched as she thrust her body up into his arms, trying to dislodge his hold. It only caused him to growl in response to her wantonness.

"I hate gowns...I think I much prefer my training clothes." Anna pouted, freeing her arms and wrapping them around his shoulders, pulling him down for a kiss. Her lips broke contact and she pushed him away when his words penetrated her mind. "Wait...why would I need a gown?"

Ben chuckled, pulling her across his lap. His hand snaked between her legs. Her eyes closed as he created friction, both her hands grasping his wrist. "It seems I know things that will make you gasp and moan, in such delightful ways..." he flicked his tongue against her neck as she shuddered in pleasure. "And you my darling, know how to make me aroused." Ben lost his words as he watched Anna ride the pleasure of his hand. She was even more exquisite in the light of day. Her body flushed with her passion, her head tossed back and her hair hanging over his arm, the tension of her muscles as she braced for her release.

"Ben..." she squeaked once her breathing had returned to normal. "Why do I need a gown? I have a bevy of dresses that the seamstress and Juta have created. I can't possibly need any more." She stood next to him in all her naked glory, her hands on her hips and her held tilted to the side. Rune points! If he looked at her any longer, he wouldn't ever leave the room.

"My darling Anna..." Ben said, standing safely at the door to her room to avoid any flailing limbs. "You need to be fit for a gown because we have a ball coming up to celebrate the engagement and the royal Garian delegation that will be arriving shortly. I'll not have you dressed as one of the servants when the Garian's arrive."

"The...engagement..." Anna looked crestfallen as she dropped her head. She nodded and turned away from him. "I understand, Your Highness."

"Anna..." It dawned on him at that moment that he hadn't explained a single thing to her. He had made plans for everything but still had yet to involve her with any of them. He was about to stride across the room when the door was yanked out of his hand.

Juta strode inside, her hands on her hips, her face scrunched up in a motherly scowl.

"Your majesty, get those lazy bones moving! Anna and I have work to do!"

· · · ·

ANNA HEARD THE DOOR close softly behind her and she dropped back into the bed, pulling the covers over her head. She grabbed the pillow and shoved her head under it, but it smelled of leather and spice and pure masculinity. Tossing it across the room, she covered her eyes with her arm. Juta yanked her out of the bed and shoved her towards the tub that was filling with steaming hot water. Anna swiped at the tears that cascaded down her face. He was engaged. She had thought by giving herself to him that he would see that she was in love with him. She had hoped that his slow and gentle way had meant he loved her as well.

Her mother Teamalah had explained thoroughly how mating happened using animals as examples, and she had even accidentally stumbled on villagers rutting while she gathered herbs in the forest. Most of those had been rough and quick. Last night he had held her, touched her, brought her to peaks of pleasure before finding his own release. She had thought that might mean something. She was a fool. He only needed her to be there to heal his kingdom and to release his power. What would he want with a thirty-eight-year-old virgin? It was a novelty. That was all.

Anna allowed Juta to plait her hair and to tug her into a gown.

"Juta...why can't the seamstress finish a seam...I mean...there are two different holes on this one..." Anna groused as she watched the two maids strip her bed. Her sheets were tossed into the fireplace. "Hey, why are you burning the sheets?"

"Anna!" Juta snapped her fingers to bring her attention to her. Once the maids had finished stripping the bedding, they disappeared from the room. "The seams have holes to accommodate knives." She watched as Anna's face lit up. "Yes child, I didn't expect you to fall back on guards to protect you. Mikal had agreed to begin your weapons training today, but he has disappeared in the night."

"Why?"

"I don't know. Now, as to your sheets, it is an old superstition of mine. We burn the sheets of first pluck to strengthen the bond of the relationship." Juta raised a brow when Anna sobbed and turned away. "Anna, stop crying. What has gotten into such a strong-willed child to turn her into a simpering fool?"

"I love him, but he doesn't love me." Anna bellowed like a fog horn. "I was just simply convenient enough to help him gain his release."

"Oh, you simple girl..." Juta sucked at her teeth and rolled her eyes. "Come over here in the light. I need to get some measurements for your gown."

"I...I prefer something simple so I can blend into the background. No need to show off that I am his doxy," she remarked as she stood in front of the window.

Juta rolled her eyes and pricked her with a pin for her comment. She took a few measurements and had her put her foot on a parchment while she traced around it. When she left the room, Anna felt the tears again. How had she gotten into such a tangled situation? She curled up in a ball in one of the wing-backed chairs by the fireplace, watching as the sheets from her bed burned down to nothing but charred embers. She shivered. It had only been a few days, but Ben could have ended up like her charred sheets. It was too close for comfort.

She wrapped her arms around her legs, resting her head on her knees. She shouldn't have allowed herself to fall in love with him. She had known from childhood that she couldn't be with him. Mikal would have been a better match for her. He was available, even if he was a prince. She scrubbed her face and huffed. There was no way she would ever fall in love with Mikal. He was loveable, but more as a brother, not as husband or lover.

Anna knew she had a choice. She could sit here the rest of the day crying about how she wanted to be Ben's wife or she could do something proactive. He had a kingdom that was dying from a blight. He wanted her to try and fix it. That meant she needed to do some research.

She rubbed her eyes and patted her hair down, making sure she looked presentable, then opened the door to her room. A young female guard stood at attention. They were only too happy to show her to the library. It was on the second floor just across from the room Ben used for training. She looked over the titles, found some that might lead her in the right direction and then settled at the table. Anna spent all day in the library, teasing out any information she could find on white rune casting and then black rune casting. It was stressfully slender on information. The tiniest bit of information she was able to tease out were things that she already knew.

The sun was just starting to sink below the window ledge when Juta finally found her. She escorted her down to the King's chamber for the evening meal. Ben's eyes fastened on her instantly as she moved to her seat. Anna picked her head up and gazed at his left ear. If she was going to be his doxy, she was going to try and enjoy the intimate contact, but she couldn't look at him. If she looked at him, her heart would break even more.

She watched as he skimmed her body with his eyes from the top of her head to the hem of her dress and back. She felt him reach out with his power, his white glow tugging against her black one. She gasped, placing her hands on either side of her trencher. He gave her a roguish smile, picking up his napkin and sitting it to the side of his plate. She tried to bury the sensual thoughts that immediately came to her mind. She had plenty of things she wanted him to do to her, now that she knew what pleasure could be found in his arms. His mind picked those thoughts out of the air and turned them into a proliferation of debauchery. Anna gasped, clutching at the table, hoping for some stability.

"Leave us..." Ben commanded the servants as they brought in the trenchers of food. They set them on the table, bowed, then backed out of the room. He repeated the command to his guard, his mental rune casting to Anna never faltering.

"Your highness..." one started to protest. The dark look he gave them sent the men scrambling from the room. Ben rose from his seat and brushed his fingers along her scarred cheek.

"Come, you look fatigued darling..." he murmured as he led her out of the dining room and to his private chamber. "I think I have just the cure."

Chapter Ten

Ben could feel Anna holding back. She was there in body and response, just not in spirit. Her body answered his every touch. He could feel as her body spasmed with delight, but something was missing. He held her against his chest, the thick blue covers pulled over them. His eyelids slowly began to drift closed when he heard her stomach growl. He chuckled, rolling out of bed to grab their food. He returned to the room and put her trencher down next to her. She pushed it to the side and ducked her head beneath her arm. He noticed she was being unusually quiet as well. In fact, the last thing he heard her say was that she understood and then she used his honorific. He put his trencher on the side of the bed and rested his head on the curve of her hip. She acted as if she was asleep, letting out a snore that he ignored. He had slept with her last night. She didn't snore when she slept.

"Anna..." She rolled onto her back, starring at the ceiling of the room.

"Anna..." he asserted more firmly. She gazed at his left ear.

"Anna!"

"What?" she squawked in annoyance.

"Where are you?" He used his thumb and forefinger to tilt her head towards him.

"I am in your bed, Your Highness, as requested."

"I..." he coughed in anger. "I am Ben, not Your Highness, not Braun, and not any other title. Is this..." he swept his hand around the bed. "Is this all because you think I am commanding you?"

"Of course..." Anna flinched as he rose above her. "That's what a good servant does, right? Tell me how to please you, Ben."

Ben jumped off the bed and paced in front of her. Displeasure poured off him in waves. Anna pressed the sheet around her shoulders and slipped out of the bed. She pushed her pain aside and reached out to him with her power. Those burning bottomless pits of seething rage turned in her direction. His anger was being aimed internally. This tall, dark, and handsome man thought that his power had made her give in to him. Anna shook her head in resignation and sighed.

"Your Majesty..." she fumbled morosely. "Ben," she corrected at his dark look. "Your power has no control over me. Go ahead...push. See if it does anything." Anna waited, saw the flash of white cross his eyes and grabbed the bedpost as images of carnal pleasure swept through her mind. He pulled back. "No, keep going. You tell me when a woman would give up and sleep with you."

Ben grabbed her free arm, eyes flashing once again, watching as the sheet dropped to the floor from the assault of carnal images that he was throwing at her. "They would have already submitted, Anna."

"I'm still standing here, not throwing myself on you." Anna fought her own response to those images, trying not to give in. His powers had nothing to do with her response. She wanted this man like she needed the blood in her veins, not because he could make her hot with need. "Your power can't make me do anything I don't want to do. I'm not like all the other women who throw themselves at you. Stop punishing yourself."

"Where are you tonight then, Anna?" he whispered, his right hand splayed across her belly, his left hand gripping the bedpost just above her, his naked and tumescent body pressed against her bottom.

"I can't be here mentally." She pressed back against him as his fingers dipped inside her slick core. She remembered her promise to herself and stiffened in his arms.

"I want all of you Anna."

"I can't give my all. You're engaged, for Gaia's sake." Tears slid down her cheeks.

"To you, Anna," he swallowed down her gasp as he cupped her breast in his hand. He kissed the tears away on her cheek and coaxed her legs apart. He teased her, pressing just to the entrance of her womanhood and then pulling back. "Only to you, my darling. I have a plan..."

Anna didn't believe him. The man hadn't asked her if she wanted to get married. He was using this as a ploy to get her in his bed and into his arms. Who was she kidding? She couldn't not be here. The first romp this evening had taken all of her determination to forget what he was doing to her, but now, she had no energy left to fight. She bent more at her waist, pressing back when he surged forward to take him inside. They both made guttural noises as he slid deep. He held still, grabbing her hips to keep her from pulling away. The need to move pulsed in their cores. Their powers reached out on the astral field and wrapped around each other. Together they sighed in contentment. When the need to move built up inside her, Anna tried to break his hold on her hips. The damn man was strong. She wiggled her bottom, clenching her abdomen muscles as she did. Ben lost his grip, his left hand shot out, catching the bedpost. Anna cried out in pleasure as his other hand dipped low once more.

"My Anna." Ben grunted with each thrust of their hips. "My love. My Anna."

Anna couldn't believe her ears. He was lost in his passion. The heat of his body against hers was unbearable. As he grasped her hips for one last thrust, she spiraled over the edge, panting heavily and holding the bedpost to stay upright. Each time this man brought her to the peak of passion she felt as if she was flying off into the ether. She was ready to crumple back into the bed and close her eyes, but Ben showed her three more times exactly how much he needed her fully present. Each time he called her his love. Each time he burned all the other thoughts out of her mind until she began to hope just a little that it was true. The last time, he rested his head against her breast and didn't move as they drifted off to sleep.

• • • •

"ANNA..." CAME THE SOFT call from the other side of the door. Anna cracked one eye open and glanced around. Ben had gotten up at some point and pulled the curtains on the bed. She was thankful for that. Anna pushed her bleary-eyed head out of the curtain and caught sight of a young serving woman. She had seen her once before, back when she had first been brought to the castle. The woman cleared her throat, her eyes averted in respect of their privacy. "Anna..."

"Yes..." Anna unwrapped her limbs from Ben, brushing a stray black lock of his hair over his forehead with a soft smile. She groped for something to cover herself and grabbed Ben's tunic. Tugging it over her head, she padded softly to the door. The maid jumped at her appearance. "Yes?"

"Uh...Juta..." the maid said something about a dress fitting and motioned towards the hall. Anna glanced out the window, noticing that the first rays of the sun had yet to come over the horizon.

Juta knew her routine. At this hour of the morning, she would be training. Anna frowned as she peeked out the hall door. She wouldn't call upon her to be at a dress fitting. There were two guards standing on the other side of the door that she didn't recognize. She moved out into the hall and peeked outside. Juta was nowhere to be seen. She turned to step back inside when someone covered her mouth and pinned her arms to her side. Anna thrashed against her attacker. She used every trick she knew and had learned from Mikal to free herself. None of them worked. She tried screaming, but the hand over her mouth prevented it. The only sounds she was able to make were muted and muffled, not even louder than a mouse squeaking.

"Keep her quiet!" the serving girl commanded in, as she pulled the door to the King's chamber closed. "You don't know what that man is capable of."

"I told you already," the man holding her grumbled. "This would have been easier weeks ago when she was still in her room. No, Zura..." he growled as they hauled her down the hallway. "You had to wait until the damn witch moved into his chamber."

"Right Cael." Zura smirked as she pried open an outer door to the courtyard. "Because I so knew that she would give in to his power last night. I had no clue how powerful the King's power was. That isn't exactly something I keep track of. Jorst! Get over here and bind her up."

Anna stopped struggling as Cael dragged her over to a horse. He removed his hand from her mouth as Jorst tied a gag around her mouth. She bit his knuckle and then screamed as loud as she could. That earned her a lovely whack to her face. Stars flashed behind her eyes, pain throbbed across her cheek, and her air was cut off for a moment as the gag was forced into her mouth. She clawed with her now free hands as the man wrapped ropes around them. She was sure she had left some bloody trails along his arms before he finished.

There was stomping and rushing behind her in the hall. The world tilted as she was lifted and tossed onto someone's lap like a sack of flour. The horse galloped away, each strike of his hoof against the ground sending pains through Anna's ribs. She wasn't sure if anyone had heard her scream. Her best chance of survival was to keep her wits about her.

Reaching out with her rune power, she tugged on Ben's power, feeling the resulting flare of passion as his power tugged back. She knew the moment he came awake, because he instantly tugged harder on her power, until they were too far apart to reach out any longer. Anna gripped the thigh of her rider tightly in her bound hands as they turned at a crazy pace. If she survived this, she promised herself she would lock herself away in a room with Ben forever and never come out.

· · · ·

"ANNA!" BEN ROARED AS he rushed naked from his chamber. His loyal guards were just now awakening. They were grasping their heads and groaning in pain. "Mikal!"

"He's still gone, your highness!" Juta replied as she came around the hall. She was clutching a tiny dwarven short sword in one hand and dwarven chain mail in the other. "She was taken by horse. Go get dressed! We can still catch them if we are fast enough."

Ben rushed back into his chamber and pulled on his breeches, tunic, and grabbed his overcoat. Returning to the hall, he greeted Juta who was now wearing her chainmail and had buckled her sword at her waist. Juta's mini horse and his black stallion were both saddled and ready when they arrived in the forecourt. Packs of provisions had been provided. He wasted no time, mounting his stallion and taking off.

He wasn't going to let anyone take her from him. That woman meant everything to him. He was so lost in his grief that he didn't pay attention to the signs he had been following. He travelled for at least an hour past where they had turned. It wasn't until Juta pulled her pony in front of his that he stopped. She berated him in dwarven.

"Use your head!" she snapped. "I haven't seen any sign of riders for an hour!"

"Dung elf!" he cried as he turned his horse and at a much slower pace began searching for signs. He reached with his power, but she was still out of range. He would find her. It didn't matter what it would take, he would turn the whole continent over to find her. When he did, he promised whoever was behind this capture would pay dearly.

Chapter Eleven

Anna kept her eyes open, looking for a moment to run. They had bound her hands and gagged her, but they had yet to tie her feet. She shivered lightly at the chill in the air. The tunic of Ben's she was wearing wasn't doing much to keep her warm. The sun was just starting to come up over the horizon.

By now, Ben would have sent the guard to find her trail. She glanced around to see if she recognized the area. They were somewhere near the river, maybe close to Amberside but that was all she could tell from her position. The riders kept up a relentless pace as they followed at a very safe distance from the river bank.

By mid-day, Anna was so exhausted and in so much pain from bouncing up and down against the hard saddle, that she closed her eyes and drifted off to sleep. She could use a nap after the lack of sleep from that night.

Did she even dare to hope that Ben truly loved her? Did she even allow that glimmer of anticipation of marriage? How would the villagers of Enderton react to having a commoner for a Queen? Did it even work like that? If he married her, would she be Queen or just the Consort? A hysterical laugh escaped her as she slid off into dreamland.

· · · ·

"ANYTHING?" JUTA DEMANDED as she took a swig of water from her waterskin. She watched as the King's eyes flashed white.

"No." He took a drink from his own waterskin and panned his gaze around the river bank. "They are still too far out of range.

Their tracks are getting harder to read. Either they have someone with them that can conceal their signs or..."

"Or they are getting closer to their destination..." Juta wiped her brow and grunted as she mounted her pony. "Let's go. No reason to stand around wondering when we could find her just behind the next bend in the river."

Ben climbed back onto his stallion. He noticed that one horse had veered off a while back, but he left that trail as it wasn't the horse that was carrying two. His best bet was to follow the horse making slightly heavier prints. That horse was either carrying a heavy load, or it was carrying two riders. He was pretty sure it was the horse carrying Anna.

The sun finally sank below the horizon and he had to stop for the night. He couldn't track horse prints in the dark, at least he was pretty sure he couldn't. Anger seethed just below the surface. Who would dare come into his kingdom, his home, and take the one thing that was most precious to him? He vowed that he wouldn't rest until that person had felt his wrath.

• • • •

ANNA FELT THE TIGHT ropes around her wrists and ankles. She couldn't get them to budge. They were cutting into her skin so tight they were cutting off her circulation. Zura, the woman who had tricked her into stepping into the hall, was sitting at a table and starring into the fire. Zura's red hair was bound up into a braid that had been wrapped around the crown of her head. She had on a long black skirt that swept the ground and hung loosely around her legs. Her gray tunic was belted around the waist with a green belt. Her black cloak lay on the back of the empty chair next to the table.

Anna watched as Zura kept rubbing her hands back and forth. Either Zura felt she was going to come into some money quickly, or she was trying to wipe the dirt of her crime away. There were soft sounds in a room just beyond her sight that she guessed were the other two kidnappers. Anna focused her power on Zura and projected the thought of loosening her bonds. Zura merely glanced in her direction, sniffed, then returned her gaze back to the fire.

Anna was beginning to feel every bruise on her torso. She wasn't sure how long she would be able to endure bouncing up and down against the saddle if she had to do it another whole day. The man that had been dressed as a guard, that Zura had called Cael, stepped inside and settled at the table with some dried meat. While they ate their meal and ignored her, Anna tried to figure out exactly what it was they wanted. She had done nothing to harm them. She was pretty sure Ben hadn't done anything either.

Ben. She closed her eyes and inhaled deeply at the sting his name conjured. His brown eyes, black hair, and masculine shaped mouth flashed in her mind and instinctively she reached out with her black rune power to see if he was near. She felt a little tingle in the pit of her stomach, but nothing else. He was still out of reach but was getting closer. Did he even know she was gone?

Yeah, she remembered that he had melded his power with hers but was that something she had dreamed or something he had actually done? She shifted on the ground, feeling the pressing need to relieve herself. Her eyes found Cael's. What did they want of her? She focused her power on him and gave him a gentle push with her power.

"Does she know?" Cael growled.

"Only what he has told her." Zura sighed and wrapped her hair around a finger. "Our king can be very persuasive when he wants to be. I would say he has fed her the lies about how much he loves her but not about the destruction he has caused."

Anna sat up straighter and leaned forward.

"Ah…" Cael smirked. "Did that get your attention little black rune caster? Yes, King Braun is a liar and a killer. Has he told you how much of our land he has killed? How the people on the border between Garia and Enderton are dying?" He watched as her eyes widened and she shook her head. "Yes…he is the one who caused it. I will bet he has been too busy wooing you over to his side that he hasn't even told you his plan to fix it. That plan uses you. He needs to drain off your power to keep the problem from getting any worse. It won't fix it. Nothing can, but he will use you as a bandage."

"She's too far gone on his power Cael." Zura rolled her eyes and stretched. "She won't believe anything you tell her."

Cael grunted, getting up to untie Anna's legs and move her outside. When they returned a few minutes later, she was tied again. Her feet throbbed as feeling slowly began to return. Cael hadn't tied her foot ropes as tight and she was thankful for that. Cael settled down at the table, watching her closely. He brushed his shaggy blonde hair out of his blue eyes and poured himself a glass of mead or wine. Anna wasn't sure what it was he was drinking from his waterskin. All she knew was the sharp tang of liquor was assaulting her nose.

"Let me tell you what happened twenty years ago." Cael took a long swallow of his drink. Zura sighed heavily, rolled her eyes, and disappeared from sight. Anna assumed there was another room with a cot. "Twenty years ago, King John had a commoner kidnapped from her home. He smuggled her across the border into Garia. While there, he had her memory wiped of his son, Prince Ben. That very same night, Prince Ben murdered his parents and set a blight upon the land in retaliation. He used his white power to turn all the soil of Enderton useless. Once thriving farms were now showing signs of pitiful harvests. Lush crops were now sprouting as if they were weeks old instead of days. The once prosperous border towns were now desperate for income. Corrupt King Ben began hunting down any casters that were powerful enough to fix his blight and killing them. He wants all the rune power for himself. He is evil...and cursed."

Anna didn't believe what he said. Ben wouldn't have killed his parents. He had loved his parents from the depth of his very soul. She tossed her power at him again. He shook his head as if warding off a bug. Then he took another swig of his liquor and laughed.

"I have been researching this blight that the Corrupt King released. He needs black rune power to control it. The only way to fix it would be to send a constant source of black power into it. That will reduce the destruction it causes, but unless you can create a big leak like he did with his power, you can only reduce it. Nothing will destroy it. I think Ben will just kill you on the spot where he released it. That will permanently decrease the destruction. How does it feel to know that the Corrupt King only cares for himself?"

Anna ignored the man. She was in love with Ben. Nothing Cael said would make her love him less. If Ben thought the only way to save his kingdom was to murder her, then he wasn't the man she was in love with. She reached out with her power, searching for him and felt her body flood with warmth as she connected. He wasn't far away. She felt relief at being rescued. She still had no clue what these two wanted with her. They only told her what they 'thought' Ben planned to do. That still left a lot of questions in her mind. She knew that Ben didn't murder his parents. It wasn't in him to do that, but what did happen? This was also the first she had heard about a blight on the land.

She thought back to the day she had purchased those carrots. Most of the vegetables in all the stalls looked much the same as those floppy carrots she had purchased. Was that what they were talking about? She heard a soft shuffle on the other side of the wall and glanced over to Cael. He was sitting with his head tossed back and soft snores coming from his throat. She wasn't sure where Zura had disappeared to. She watched as the front door slowly opened and a small body slipped inside.

Tears slipped from her eyes as Juta cut her bonds and slipped the gag off her mouth. Anna let out a heavy sigh of relief and worked the feeling back into her hands. The tingling had already started in her feet earlier and was now becoming slightly bearable. Juta held the door open and motioned for her to slip out. Trying to be as quiet as possible, she crawled on her hands and knees to the door and shimmied through, right into the arms of Ben. He swept her off her hands and knees and into his arms faster than she could inhale. The scent of leather and spice filled her senses and her body forgot how sore it was.

When he finally released her and stood her on her feet, she assumed they would climb on his horse and head back to the castle. Instead, Ben kissed her, pushed her towards Juta, and turned to the house with his sword in hand. Anna reached out and caught his arm, shaking her head. Irritation flared up inside him and she used her power to push tranquil thoughts to him. He wavered for a moment, his sword dropping from the ready position. She had almost won him over to her side when the door opened and Cael cursed loudly. The sound of metal clanging against metal rang through the air as Ben parried an attack. Anna didn't want to watch. She knew with the fury boiling in his veins that Ben wouldn't stop until Cael was dead. But she couldn't look away either.

"Ah...never worry," Juta sniffed with begrudging admiration in her native dwarven tongue. "I taught him everything I know. This ruffian won't best him."

"I'm not worried about that." Anna replied back in dwarven. "I'm more worried about the damage he will take while doing it."

"My child..." Juta snickered. "You know my language very well! Where, pray tell have you learned it?"

"I know many languages, Juta. When you spend twenty years running for your life, you learn to pick up a thing or two." Anna flinched when Cael punched Ben in the face. He was going to have a nice shiner in the morning. "You never really talk much around me. I just assumed you were a quiet dwarf. Although that seemed unlikely as I have yet to meet a dwarf who hasn't loved to spin yarns of days long past."

"Well, when we get you back to the castle, I will be happy to spin any yarn you want. Did these two kidnappers tell you what they wanted?"

"There were three and no." Anna shook her head as Ben successfully swiped Cael off his feet. He stood above him with his sword pointed at his throat. That was when Ben did something she hadn't expected. He sheathed his sword, helped the man up, and then tied his hands behind his back. She felt her chest swell with pride and love, her power hugging his. He turned and gave her a wink before stepping into the hovel they had sheltered her in. He returned empty handed. "There was no one else inside?"

"No." Ben wiped the sweat from his brow and tethered Cael's horse to his own. He brought the second horse over and tossed a threadbare blanket over the saddle. Gently he handed Anna up into the saddle. "There was no one else inside, so his accomplice has fled."

"That's fine. I've seen her in the castle."

"Child...which girl was it?" Juta demanded.

"Zura." She looked at the man on horseback and pointed to him. "That's Cael. There was a third man they called Jorst."

"Jorst?" Ben snapped. His eyebrows rose as he climbed on his horse and turned in the direction of the castle. "He had better make sure he is well and completely gone before I find him."

"You know him?" Anna inquired.

"He was part of my personal guard." Ben allowed his horse to pick the path through the forest. Since it was still full dark, it wasn't wise to push them any faster than they wanted to go. "Cael, would you like to tell me exactly why you thought kidnapping my love was a good idea?"

Ben's question was met with only silence. He snorted and turned back to watching Anna as her horse plodded along in front of him. She was wearing only his tunic. As enticing and erotic as that was, he was sure she would be freezing. After holding her close, he felt the warmth from her and knew his power was warming her. Sometimes he felt as if his power was more of a curse, but tonight he knew it could also be a blessing. He had only lost two days hunting for Anna. He still had plenty of time to figure out what he was going to do at the ball.

He wouldn't marry the new Garian princess. He would rather die. Anna was the woman he was going to marry. That meant he had to find another way to make a peace treaty with Garia. He rubbed his face wearily, feeling a sudden sense of peace wash over him. When he looked up, Anna was looking back at him with a soft understanding smile on her face. Yeah, he would rather kill himself before marrying that sniveling woman they called the Garian princess. It was Anna or nothing now.

Chapter Twelve

Anna inhaled deeply and wrapped her arms tighter around the masculine body next to her. Once they had returned to the castle, Cael had been thrown in the dungeon and Ben had decree that no one was to interrupt him for the next two days except to bring food. She had laughed at him, but he picked her up and tossed her over his shoulder, ending any argument as he carried her into his private chambers.

He showed her multiple times how much he cherished her, missed her, loved her during the course of that first day. The second day they had spent most of the day sleeping. She was content at the moment just to be held in his arms. She was still sore from being tossed around like a toy on Cael's lap and being poked by the saddle horn in the ribs, but she didn't care. She was alive and wrapped up in her comfort spot.

She felt Ben run his finger down her scared cheek. Reflexively she flinched away, turning her head into his chest. He stuck his finger under her chin and tried to force her eyes to look at him. She pulled out of his grasp and buried her face again. Anna felt him move his fingers to a more sensitive area and she snarled, nipping his shoulder as she wrapped her legs around him to stop his foraging.

"A little cranky this morning darling?" he teased. His finger ran along the scar again and he exhaled a deep breath. "Where did you get this?"

"Why on my cheek, Your Highness!" she giggled as his hands played along her sides.

"Anna..." He watched her playful doe-colored eyes turn dark and skitter away from him.

"It was a long time ago."

"How long?"

"Twenty years." She shot a quick glance at him and saw the darkness creep into his face. She untangled her body from him and rolled out of bed. "It is in the past Ben. Leave it there. Nothing good has ever come from digging up the past."

"I beg to differ..." Ben caught her around the waist, and nipped her ear as he held her against his body. "I spent twenty years looking for my past and I finally have her in my arms."

"That's..." Anna sniffed indignantly and turned in his arms. "That's a little different. Come on Ben...you have plenty of duties that you need to attend to. I am sure I have plenty of things Juta needs me for. Besides, at some point you are going to have to tell me what has happened to your kingdom so I can try to help you fix it."

"Right...didn't you just say that I should leave things in the past?" He scooped her up and carried her back to the bed, snuggling down with her in his arms. "Why should I dig up my past when you won't dig up yours?"

"Point taken..." Anna conceded and gave him a little peck on the neck as she snuggled closer to his warm body. "Well, if you really must know. Your father did it. He thought maybe it was my looks that had you ensorcelled. He said this way you wouldn't know me when you saw me again. He also figured it would make me ugly enough to keep you from desiring me. I think his biggest fear was losing you to the dark side of your power. I have to admit, I was a little afraid of that myself. I had felt your power slipping once and wasn't sure if anyone would be strong enough to control you."

"You are..." he pointed out dryly. Hatred at what his father had done filled him as he held her close. The fact that she calmly gave him the story did little to ease his pain.

"I am now...but that night..." Anna traced a design on his chest. "I am not sure anyone was, Ben. Your power was so strong that night and I was so susceptible at the time..."

"Yet you still rejected my power." Ben tilted her face up and he kissed the tip of her nose. "You shouldn't ever doubt how strong you are."

"You can remind me." Her fingers stopped tracing circles on his chest and she raked her nails along his skin until he hissed. "I shared...your turn. Probably should start with the rumor of murdering your parents."

"Ah..." he caught her fingers and tugged them away from the angry red marks she had left. "You've heard that one, huh? I guess you could say in a way I did murder my parents, but not by my hand, only by my actions."

"How?" she kissed the marks on his chest and retrieved her hand to continue running it across his chest.

"When my father told me that he was going to banish you from Enderton, I became enraged. My power was already heightened by our encounter. It began to surge. Mother grabbed me and fled the castle. She rode out into the woods not far from here and tried to help contain my power with hers. She ended up having a heart attack. My powers began to spin out of control." He shuddered as he remembered that moment. "The only thing I could think of, was to gather my errant power and shove it into the ground. I kept gathering and shoving, hoping that it would stop growing but the grief of losing my mother, losing you, and my anger at my father for what he had done kept feeding it. Since my white rune power feeds off emotions more than most rune powers, it built into an almost living thing. I called it a blight because it turned all the plants in the area black."

"All of them?"

"Every last shred of that forest was turned. The next morning when I awoke, I found my mother still dead, the forest dead around me, and my power still morphing and growing. I was frightened and unsure of what to do. Juta found me. She had been mother's seamstress. When she couldn't find mother, she went looking for her. She found me in that clearing, dropped down to her knees and taught me how to channel and focus using meditation. She saved me. The meditation calmed my emotions and together we brought my mother back to the castle for burial. That afternoon a guard from a border town came riding into the courtyard with my father's body. He reported that he had been caught in an earthquake and a tree had fallen on him. Before anyone could get to him, he had succumbed and passed. I made myself an orphan."

"If it was a random earthquake, how in the world do you think that you caused his death?"

"Funneling my power into the ground had created some form of fungus that attacks plants. It set off a ricochet of power as it grew exponentially, causing storms, lighting, earthquakes, and even random funnel clouds. I know this for a fact." He closed his eyes at the harrowing experience that was replaying behind his eyelids. "I spent that whole week listening to reports from farms and villages. Thankfully, it didn't happen anywhere past the border, so Garia didn't take offense and attack."

"Well..." Anna sat up, wrapping her arms around her knees. She looked down at him as his hand stroked her lower back. "The way I see it Ben, you didn't murder your parents. The blight was a byproduct of your power surging out of control, not an open act against a human being. That means..." She straddled his waist and bent down to kiss him. "You are not the Corrupt King everyone is calling you. I will solve your problem and you can live happily ever after with your Princess of Garia."

"No." Ben pushed her off his waist and crawled out of the bed. "I am never going to marry her. It may be beneficial for my kingdom, but I can't marry her." He scooped her up and carried her to the dining area where there was a light lunch set out. "I told you that I love you and that I am going to marry you. There is no question about it. If that means I need to step down as King, so be it."

"Maybe the Princess of Garia would be better suited to Mikal?" Anna teased. She watched as he dropped the carrot he was eating.

"That might work..." he guffawed. "The problem is getting him to agree."

"Excuse me, Your Highness!" Juta said softly as she peeked into the dining room. She caught sight of bare skin and kept herself on the other side of the door respectfully.

"Juta...I believe I said two days. The sun hasn't risen on the morrow yet..." he growled.

"I know, Your Highness, but...I think you really need to know that a delegation from Garia has arrived ahead of schedule."

"Really?" he rolled his eyes and glanced at Anna with a devious smile. "How many?"

"Uh...six of them, the Princess included..."

"Very well, Juta." Ben popped the carrot into his mouth and chewed, watching Anna as she continued to eat delicately and quietly. "Clear Anna's things out of the purple suite and put them in my chambers. Give the delegation the rooms along that hall. The princess should definitely have the chambers right next to mine. Give her the red suite."

"Yes, Your Highness." Juta chuckled herself as she pulled the door closed a little more.

"And Juta..." he waited, hearing the footsteps return. "I mean two full days..."

"Understood. I shall handle it from here."

"You should probably go deal with them instead of sitting in here all day," Anna yawned and stretched. Already she could hear thumping as trunks and cases were brought down the hallway. She watched as a hungry look passed over Ben's face. She felt his power flare as he watched her. Desire clawed in her belly as he advanced towards her. "We really shouldn't do that...not with the Princess next door," she pleaded, swallowing hard as he tugged her out of the seat.

"Yeah, probably not." His mouth pressed against hers. He felt her resolve hold for just a minute, then it crumbled. Her arms wrapped around his shoulders, her right leg hooked his waist, her hips pressed against his. "Although I am sure she can't hear us."

"If you are sure..."

Anna inhaled deeply as he wrapped her hair around his hand and tugged her head back. His lips and tongue made a trail of fire along her jaw and down her neck. She vaguely heard the sound of their food and eating things falling to the floor. Then she was on her back, her legs locked firmly around his hips. She whimpered, her fingers running through his hair, trying to pull him to her for another kiss. His mouth was working along her torso, suckling her breasts, his hands pinning her down. She pressed her hips against him. He only moved further down her body. His tongue dipped in and out of her belly button. She felt his teeth nip lightly at the fold there. She moved her hands out of his hair and grabbed his arms. She ran them along the length of his powerful shoulders and biceps, urging him to move lower. His mouth finally nudged her open, delving into her moist folds. She groaned loudly, thrusting her hips up. His fingers and mouth worked magic, making her forget everything that was happening. She grasped the edge of the table as she worked her hips back and forth. The rasp of his beard made her pant until finally she shouted his name with her release.

Ben worked his way back up, capturing her lips in a salty kiss. She smiled, flipping him onto the table next to her and then jumping down. She reversed their positions, watching as his toes curled, the muscles in his calves tightened, and his hips bucked when her mouth encircled that pulsing member. She took every inch of him inside her mouth, working her lips up, then she nipped his tip and heard him groan. The smack of his hands as he grabbed the edge of the table were satisfying. She continued her assault, grasping his hips as he bucked against her. He eventually caught her hair and stopped her, panting heavily. Anna looked deep into those pools of desire and smiled as he tugged her back onto the table with him. She straddled his waist, sighing with gratification as he pushed inside and all the way to her core.

"I love you..." he growled, thrusting up against her. The table rocked and thumped with his movements. Her eyes darkened; her mouth opened in an 'oh' of desire. He grasped her hips, pumping harder. "Ah Goddess, I love you, Anna."

"I love you Ben..." she moaned as her body tightened and released. He pressed into her hard one more time, his warm desire flooding through her body. She rested her head against his as they lay there spent.

"You mean it?" he begged as his arms tightened around her.

"Yes. I...I love you, but I also know you are a King and have a country to run. If you must marry the Princess of Garia, you must do it."

"I am going to marry you." He picked her up as his breathing returned slowly to normal and carried her into the bedroom. "I hope the Princess heard every thump and bump, because I'm going to show you the rest of the night how much we belong together!" he growled in her ear as he pressed her against the far wall of the bedroom.

"Show me again..." she breathed against his lips.

Chapter Thirteen

Ben sat on the throne and watched with a yawn hidden behind his hand as the Garian delegation paraded into the room. There were musicians playing music, gymnasts doing flips and flops, there was even a jester parading around as the three men strutted slowly into the room one by one, taking up seats on the first row of benches. Two women followed them, taking the daintiest steps he had ever seen. They joined the men on the bench, leaving a large opening for one person in the middle.

He turned his gaze back to the doorway as the Princess finally stepped inside. Her honey blonde hair was teased out into some large hairdo with her tiara in the middle. He noticed that there was probably six inches of some gunk on her face. She had been painted up to look like a doll. Her bright vivid blue eyes were wide and round as she stepped into the room. The princess was probably around five foot and the heels she was wearing made her approximately five feet three inches. Her dress was pink, done up in the current fashion with hoops and whatnot making it seem as if she was ten foot wide. He watched as she shuffled down the aisle to the end where his crier announced her.

"Presenting Princess Elena of Garia."

Elena dipped a curtsy, her enormous skirt wobbling back and forth like a bell. When he motioned towards her, she rose, her tiara moving precariously on top of that mound of hair. She batted her eyes at him as she moved as slowly as possible to the open spot on the front bench between her servants. The hall got quiet, waiting for him to proclaim something, to speak, to move. He only watched the door, waiting.

Murmurs started in the back and began to increase in volume until he broke out in a sloppy grin. Anna had stepped into the doorway. More likely Anna was pushed from behind. He could see Juta jumping to the side out of sight. Anna's eyes skittered around nervously until she caught his gaze. She thrust her head up slightly higher, her shoulders squared, her back straightened. She didn't break eye contact as she walked down the aisle just as Princess Elena had.

Anna's hair had been combed back into a dwarven knot at the nape of her head. Juta had tucked some stones into her hair and they glinted in the light. Her neck had been adorned with a simple necklace that had once been his mothers. It was just large enough to catch the light and wink at him from the midst of her cleavage. He enjoyed the look of this new gown that Juta had created. It was in the style of his kingdom, showing off her belly, lower back, shoulders, and most of her chest. The skirt was loose around her body but clung to her hips and thighs, just barely brushing the floor. The whole outfit was black and stitched with white embroidery. Her feet were encased in a pair of soft black doeskin boots.

"Presenting, Anna Forsooth of Enderton."

Anna reached the end of the walk and dipped into a more perfect curtsy than the Princess had. When he motioned for her to rise, she did so without wobbling, her gaze never leaving his as she turned and started to walk to the other set of benches. He cleared his throat and watched as she cringed slightly, her head dipping closer to her shoulders, but she turned, taking the steps regally until she clasped her hand in his and turned to face everyone in the room. Her eyes instantly fell on the pink cloud to her left. The Princess' face seemed fairly impassive, but when Anna reached out with her power, she caught jealousy, hatred, and deviousness. She pulled her power back quickly, not liking the slimy feeling the contact left. Ben tugged her hand and she took a step forward as he spoke to the assembled court.

"Anna Forsooth has been pardoned of all her crimes against the crown. Let it be known on this day that I fully intend to make Anna Forsooth Queen Consort. If any oppose this, they shall have audience with me during the remainder of this week. At the end of the week, we shall have a ball to celebrate my engagement. Tonight, we will feast the arrival our friends of the Garian delegation." He gripped her hand. She turned to him, ducking her head in a nod, a brief glimpse of nerves showing in her gaze. "No nerves darling. You are a rock." He led her the few steps back to his throne and waited as she sat on the smaller one next to him before resuming his seat.

Anna sat ramrod straight on the smaller throne, thankful it had a little padding and wasn't completely uncomfortable. Ben never released her hand, so she gripped it as tightly as she could without telling the world how uncomfortable she was. She took a mental spin around the room, checking out the emotions of his court. Most of them seemed elated that he had finally settled on someone. There were a few broken hearts. She assumed those were the few women he had used at some point to release his power.

She felt confusion from the two female delegates that had come with the Garian Princess. The three men were perplexed but also resolved. She could almost sense something sinister going through their brains, but she just couldn't grasp exactly what it was. There was one very angry man in the back. From this distance, she couldn't tell if they were friend or foe. She pushed a little serenity in his direction and felt that anger subside into fear. That was a strange response. She shifted her gaze to Juta who was beaming at her like a proud mother from the back of the room.

Anna sent Juta a feeling of unease and then carefully adjusted her gaze to the man in the back. When she returned her eyes to Juta, she was moving in the direction of the man. What a relief to know that she could use her power for more than just stealing children and smuggling them into Garia. She focused back on Princess Elena. She was decked out in baubles that were worth a fortune. Her tiara looked as if it would fall off her head with one wrong move. It had the largest diamond at the top in the middle, making it wobble every time she moved.

The men sitting around her were no better, Anna thought as she raised a brow slightly. She couldn't make any major moves that anyone would see. She didn't want them to think she was for or against anything happening as she wasn't even listening. The male delegation was decked out in the latest fashion, made mostly from silks, with delicate laces tucked here and there. Anna wondered how much these royals spent on themselves and how much they spent on their people. She shuddered as she got a close-up picture. She had been stealing the children out of Enderton and taking them across the border. Here in Enderton, they had feared for their lives, but what was it like for them in Garia?

She knew they could use their rune casting in Garia with no penalty. She also knew there were plenty of teachers that showed them how to harness their powers, but was that the only reason to move them. She thought back to the day she had been captured, remembering how Ben had said Jakob needed to get strong and return back to him as a warrior. What did that mean? Did Ben have more of a plan together than she was aware of?

She felt her cheeks start to warm. Her thighs clenched together. Liquid heat began to pool in her most intimate spot. Shifting her gaze back out to the world instead of her own mind, she realized that Ben was stroking her fingers. He was obviously just as bored with this as she was. She snapped her power at him and he straightened slightly, coughing lightly behind his hand, wrapping his fingers through hers once more.

"Thank you Arant." Ben rumbled. He stood and she stood beside him, just a few steps behind and to the side. "Prisoner Cael Trailwinder, you have been found guilty of kidnapping, plotting against the crown, and endangering the future Queen Consort. For your crimes, you shall be condemned to rot in the dungeon until such time as I feel you have repaid your debt to my kingdom. Arant, please escort him back to his cell."

Anna exhaled softly. He could have punished him by death. Although an indeterminate amount of time in the dungeon could also result in death. She shuddered slightly, remembering how damp and dank those cells were. She would give him a week and then remind Ben that he was down there. She couldn't allow him to perish in that manner. She caught a stray feeling of harmful intent from someone in the hall and she tried to use her power to pinpoint it.

"That will be enough court for today." Ben wrapped her arm around his and led her off the dais and out of the hall. She still wasn't able to pinpoint that odd harmful feeling. When he opened a door and pushed her inside, she was too distracted to notice they were in his study. "You are breathtaking in that outfit..." he growled, his mouth devouring hers.

"Ben..." she snipped as she fought against his hold. "I'd love for you to rip this constraining fabric from my body." He caught her mouth again with excited greed. "But there is someone out there who means you or I harm." She gripped his arms as he had her bent over backwards. His body stilled and she relaxed as he slowly stood.

"You know because..."

"I caught their emotions. It was just as we walked out of the hall but I couldn't pinpoint it."

"When I made my announcement about you being my Queen Consort...did you read the delegation?" Ben settled into the chair behind his desk. He watched as she paced back and forth, her brow wrinkled in puzzlement.

"Yes. The Princess was of course angry and jealous, but she was also planning something, something that felt slimy. The two women that were with her were just confused. The three men however were perplexed but also resolved. I didn't get a pure harmful intention until we left. Did Cael have any family?"

"Maybe..." Ben shrugged, shuffling parchments from one side of his desk to the other. "I didn't really check. I am not in the habit of notifying the next of kin when I sentence a person for attacking me or my consort."

"I'll have to..." Anna stopped as Juta entered the room. Juta smiled at her as she motioned for her to come closer. Ann stepped over, then instantly regretted it. Juta wrapped her short stubby hands around her legs and squealed. "Juta, stop..." she remarked, instantly switching over to dwarven.

"You were perfect my beautiful child." Juta pulled back, swiping a tear from her eye and glancing over at Ben. He was shaking his head but smiling. "I can't wait to see you in the ball gown or your bridal gown! Oh, your Bridal Gown...I have just the plan...I can get that down on parchment now, yes! You come with me and I will tell you the tale of my parents' wedding. You'll be sobbing by the time..."

"Stop." Anna commanded again. "Did you check that guy out?"

"Ah...yes." Juta sniffled again, tucking her hair back behind her ear. "He was angry and afraid that with you as a consort, the King would start enslaving his people. He also figured with Ben outlawing rune casting that he was going to use you as a hunter of their people."

"What is this?" Ben demanded, leaning forward as Juta explained. "When did this happen?"

"It was during the whole boring trial for Cael, right before you started losing interest. I caught his anger while I was scanning the crowd and sent Juta to check it out."

"Proudly I can say I didn't see you move one muscle..." he complained dryly. "You'll make a perfect consort."

"She sent it through her emotions and eyes..." Juta laughed, holding her stomach as she moved to the door. "Dung elf...you act like you don't know how to use your own powers..."

"Anna..." Ben glared as Juta left and closed the door. "When were you going to tell me that."

"That wasn't the problem. Anger is one thing, but harmful intent and deviousness are different. The first one means you are going to explode and then settle down. The second two are long time simmers that are potentially deadly or dangerous and usually don't ever go away."

"Right." He caught her arm as she began pacing again and pulled her behind the desk. Once she was settled on his lap with her head against his shoulder, he let out a contented sigh. "First...remember that as King, someone is ALWAYS intent on harming me. Second...as my newly announced future Queen Consort, you will ALWAYS have someone intent on harming you."

"Like your former lovers?" she suggested, tugging on his jacket.

"I may have had a few before I was twenty..." he admitted, feeling her tense slightly. "But after I cornered you in the forest and the whole world went topsy turvy, I haven't had a single one. It has only been you since that day, Anna."

"Right..." Anna snarked drily. "What's the other items?"

"Other items?" He tilted his head and snuggled her hips tighter against his lap. "We were listing things?"

"First...someone is always intent on harming you..." she remarked sarcastically in her best imitation of him.

"Oh...yeah." Ben tried to pull that train of thought back into his brain. It wasn't easy with her half clad in that sexy outfit sitting on his lap. "Third, you need to learn about all of this." He motioned to the mountain of parchment on the desk.

"Ben, I think we should talk about..."

"We will let Mikal handle it when he gets back. It's what he is good at. Now, let me show you the ledgers..."

Chapter Fourteen

A royal feast to welcome the Garian delegation was nothing like Anna had pictured it to be. The main hall had been transformed from an empty space with sparring equipment and a few random braziers into an opulent eating hall. The walls had been covered in obsidian black and snowy white silks tied together with navy blue cords. Bouquets of wild flowers had been arranged artfully in large stone pots. The flowers appeared to be lilies, lavender, jasmine, and some sweat peas. This close to the end of summer she had to wonder where they were able to get all the flowers.

More braziers had been brought in from other places in the castle and placed strategically along the sides of the room to provide more lighting. In the back of the room near the doors was a small raised platform where several men and women were creating the most breathtaking serene music she had ever heard. She turned as her eyes followed the rows of tables up to the front of the hall where another raised platform covered the whole area. The table would be large enough to seat the Garian delegation, Ben, Mikal, his head of security and her. She gulped as she thought about sitting in front of all the people in this room.

"Worried about sitting in front of all of these people?" Juta remarked in her native tongue as she leaned jauntily against the door. Juta had her long blonde hair loose around her face, waving down her back with a few sprigs of flowers tucked into the strands. Her gray eyes held a hint of mirth but also the intelligence that Juta had been hiding since Anna had come to the castle.

"Yes," Anna admitted, her cheeks flushing red as she scanned the room. Servants were setting trenchers and utensils onto the hand carved mahogany tables. The trenchers and utensils were all gold at the head table and then wooden with gilt edging on the tables below the dais. Fine linens of black and white were spread out alternatively at each seat. "I haven't a clue what Ben is thinking. I couldn't possibly fit in up there..."

"You will fit in just fine..."

"I won't." Anna glanced at her hands and sighed. "Look at these hands. These are the hands of a woman who spent her whole life toiling in dirt to help her family or climbing trees to evade guards. They look nothing like Princess Elena's hands. My poor rough hands will snag those fine linens the moment I put them on my lap."

"Nonsense." Juta sniffed and pushed off the wall. "Have you ever looked at Ben's hands child? His hands are just as work roughened as yours."

"I..." she paused for a moment as she thought of the feel of those hands against her skin and sighed as her cheeks warmed again. "Sure, but he is the King. That is expected of him..."

"No, not really. His hands should be exactly like Princess Elena's." Juta sucked on her teeth and sighed, catching Anna's hand and tugging her out of the hall. "Come child, we need to prepare you for the feast. I have just the gown to make everyone gasp in awe of you."

Anna allowed Juta to tug her to Ben's royal bedchamber. Ben followed the two with his eyes as he sat at his desk working through a pile of missives. Once inside the dressing chamber, two other maids appeared to assist with getting her dressed. After taking a quick bath, the two maids waved stiff boards near her hair while

Juta lathered her up with some type of cream that smelled delightfully of lavender. She allowed the ladies to dress her in a purple, black, and white outfit that shimmered just so in the light.

She marveled at how silky the material was as she was pushed down onto a small stool. Both of the ladies worked on wrapping black ribbons around her legs and fastening a pair of soft but firm leather pieces to her feet with the ribbons. It was a cute creation and Anna caught herself chuckling as she thought of running in these slippers. The ribbons would shred and the leather would fall off within at least a few minutes.

"Juta!" Ben called from the door to the chamber. Juta had just finished weaving some white ribbons into her hair. The quick sucking in of air made Anna jump from the stool and whirl around, prepared to fight if she had to when she caught sight of Ben's astonished face.

"I know..." Juta smirked. "I am very good at what I do."

"Always humble Juta." Ben cleared his throat and held his arm out for Anna. "You are breathtaking in that outfit and I would hate to have to share you, but..." he murmured as they walked out of his personal chambers. "We do have a delegation to feed and make merry with."

"I am not sure Princess Elena will want to make merry with me...or you for that matter..." Anna whispered as they took the last step up the stairwell and moved towards the hall.

What had been an empty hall while she had been checking it out was now full of the nobles of Enderton, the higher-level peasants, and the Garian delegation. Anna inhaled deeply, counting to ten as the whole room of people turned as they entered the room. Ben and Anna were introduced by the crier as they stepped through the door. She watched as several women and men tucked their faces behind their hands and began to whisper. She immediately straightened her back and held herself taller as he walked her to the front of the room and seated her at the head table on his right.

Ben stood, looking out at the crowd of people, waiting as the whispering slowly died down. Raising his hand, he gestured at the back of the room. Servants began to file in from the outside staircase with trays heavy with food. She watched as they sat the trays on their table and then on the tables below them. When the covers were lifted, Anna found her eyes growing wide. She had never seen so much food in one place.

A pit roasted pig sat in front of Ben along with two roasted pheasants, a bunch of salted fish, and some seared beef. She watched as more servants brought more trays. These held steamed vegetables, roasted vegetables, raw vegetables, and soft fluffy rice. Another servant placed several linen wrapped baskets on the table between each of the guests.

Ben caught her hand as she slowly reached to peel back a linen on one of the baskets. He pulled that hand up and gave it a soft kiss, then wrapped his fingers with hers and sat it on the table in full view of Princess Elena on his left. He gave Anna a soft loving smile and a small shake of his head as yet another servant arrived and filled their cups with liquid. She was pleased that hers was filled with grape juice and not with liquor.

A person whispered behind her softly, causing her to jump in her seat. Her eyes quickly scanned the room to see if anyone had noticed. The servant behind her had inquired what she wanted to eat. She noticed that there was another behind Ben making the same inquiry. Following his lead, she whispered softly that she would like some fish, steamed vegetables, and a little rice. The servant filled her trencher with the items she had requested, peeling back the linen covered basket and presenting warm bread to her as well.

When she nodded in acceptance, he picked pieces of food out with a small utensil, tasted them, rolling the food around on his tongue, then swallowing. Satisfied, he settled her trencher in front of her and disappeared back into the hidden shadows.

"One would think..." Princess Elena remarked dryly as her own member of her delegation had completed this task for her. "That you would know not to eat something before it was tasted first." She sniffed and glanced over at her delegation, letting out a light chuckle as the other members tittered behind their linens. "After all, with such a recent decree of becoming the King's Consort, one might just consider how many would try to poison them."

"Really?" Anna let her eyes widen with the appropriate amount of fear and surprise. "Huh, I guess I never thought of that." She rubbed the scar on her face and smiled sweetly at the woman, raising a brow as she sipped lightly at her juice and then saluted her with the cup. "Since I have already survived one attempt on my life, I would never have dreamed of someone being dense enough to try again."

Princess Elena huffed in indignation while Ben only chuckled heartily. He waved his hand and the servants began to vanish as the guests all began to serve themselves and eat. Nerves fluttered in Anna's gut as she picked lightly at the food in front of her. She took this moment to study Princess Elena's change of outfit. The pink nightmare she had been dressed in had been swapped for a Garian style red fitted dress. The skirt ended just above her knee and clung tightly to her thighs and hips. It was a wonder she was able to walk with the fabric that tight. Her tunic, while loose around her shoulders, was skin tight around her waist. Her legs were adorned with footwear much the same as what Anna was currently wearing, only in red. Her long blonde hair had been washed and combed out of the cloud it had been in. Now it waved gently down her back with red sparkling jewels tucked into it like a net. The face paint had been washed off and had been reapplied with a little more elegance. The overall affect was appealing to a lot of the men in the room as Anna scanned the crowd. She caught sight of more than a few that were sending frank appraisals at Elena.

"...I would be surprised one of such low born stature could ever understand the significance of King Braun's decree..."

"Beg pardon!" Ben snapped just as Anna was studying the Garian Prime Minister. There was something off about the direction of his thoughts. She did not have the power to read his mind but the emotions she caught were not normal. She returned her attention to the conversation. "You are a guest in my kingdom. To insult..."

"Please Bennie, dear..." Princess Elena cut him off with a pout. She placed her soft hand on his arm and batted her eyes at him. "One cannot insult someone of inferior intellect, especially when that inferior intellect is busy with roaming eyes."

Ben snatched his arm out of her grasp, seething with anger. "Anna..." he started.

"Yes?" Anna spoke up, her eyes wide and innocent. "My apologies, Your Highnesses!" She dipped her gaze to her trencher and sighed. "I am afraid my mind wandered for a moment."

"I was just explaining to my Bennie here, that..."

"Enough for the informal address!" he snarled softly.

"Fine." Princess Elena huffed. "I was just explaining to King Braun that you could not possibly fathom the impact his decree to make you the Queen Consort would have on his kingdom."

"Oh..." Anna giggled and hid her face behind her linen. Her eyes snapped over to Ben and she pushed her black rune power towards his white, snuggling it against the orb, calming his irritated nerves. "I see." She nibbled lightly at the salted fish, tilted her head to the side for a moment of contemplation, then sighed. "No, I guess you would be right Princess Elena. One of such low born stature, like myself, could not possibly fathom the implication of a King taking a peasant to be his wife. Especially, not with that kingdom being pressed into the decision to marry the bordering kingdom's delightfully perfidious princess, all for the sake of land that doesn't belong to either party. Also, in retrospect, his decision to marry a peasant that holds all the traits of a rune caster in a kingdom where he has decreed that no rune casters shall be permitted, would make all future decisions shaky at best." She shrugged, raised a brow, then tipped her cup in the direction of the princess. "I guess we just have to trust that King Braun has a fantastic reason for his decision. I mean, after all...my ugly scarred face couldn't hold a flame to your overt beauty. Maybe his attraction to me is more than just looks?" With a wink, Anna squeezed Ben's hand, then returned her gaze to the Prime Minister.

"How dare..."

"Might I remind you..." Ben coughed with a smirk. "You started this conversation."

"Well..." Princess Elena stood in a huff, tipping slightly to the side as she tried to take a step too large for the constraints of her skirt. "I have never been more insulted in my life. I think I have enjoyed enough hospitality of this court for one evening.

Good night, Bennie dear. Let us hope that you see reason in the morning."

"Perhaps." Ben tipped his head with a smirk as the entire Garian delegation rose and disappeared from the hall. The conversations grew louder and happier once the last of them had filed out of the room. Anna let out a relieved sigh as she furrowed her brow in thought. "That was...interesting." He tilted his head as he studied her. "I swear just when I think I have figured everything out about you, you present another side. Where did you learn to gracefully handle a conversation like that?"

"I...uh..." Anna scrunched up her nose and shrugged her shoulders. "I know a lot of things."

"Do you know how to solve our blight situation?"

"I have been reading the books in the library but there is very slim information on our powers."

"My mother..." Ben started, rubbing his thumb along her fingers as she gracefully began her meal. "She once told me that our powers were much more than just thinking things. There was a written system of runes that could be used to enhance our powers. It was also rumored that there were powerful gems that could be used. When the original Corrupt King became powerful and began his rampage, all those books on runes and stones were destroyed to keep him from gaining more control. Now, all we have are the few slim volumes that describe what each of the powers can do."

"Forbidden runes, huh?" Anna scrunched up her nose and winked at him. "Sounds slightly familiar." She bumped his shoulder lightly with hers. "I guess we will have to check out your blight and try things out until we can figure out what will solve it."

"Your intelligence, my stubbornness, Astrid's knowledge, and Mikal's tenacity..." Ben grinned. "I am sure between the four of us we could eventually figure something out."

"Then you will have to take me to the forest where you started the blight. First though, I think I need to finish off this food. I am famished."

Chapter Fifteen

Ben had been holding private audiences with everyone from his court all week. He had stated that the audiences should be for those who were opposed to him wedding Anna. Strangely, the Garian delegation had asked for a private audience only on the last day. He planned on speaking with them first thing in the morning over breakfast but duty had called. The rest of his court used those private audiences to congratulate him and try to pry his plans for the Garian delegation from him. He had just closed the door on his last private audience of the day when he caught the hint of lilacs and lavender. Turning, he watched Anna slip inside the study. She was holding two staffs and was dressed in the exercise clothes that Juta had designed for her. Ben stripped off his coat, his vest, his shirt and then removed his boots and socks. It would be such a relief to blow off some steam and get a workout in.

He had been working with Anna in the morning on a few simpler routines with the staffs, but hadn't gone into any major work. He was still waiting for Mikal to return so he could take over the more detailed precision with edged weapons. After all, Mikal was the better swordsman and had taught him everything he knew. He followed behind Anna, enjoying the sway of her wide hips. She had the most perfect curve in her lower back. His hand fit perfectly in that sweet indent. He moved just a little faster, settling his hand in that spot and enjoying the warmth that spread from her body to his. All it took was a touch and he could feel Anna's desire flare to life. Truthfully, all it really took was a look or a thought that she could catch and her mind was filled with just as many images as his was. He swallowed a laugh, not wanting her to know which direction his thoughts were going. Ben had walked only five steps into the hall that was starting to be decorated for the ball when he felt something sting the back of his neck.

"Ow..." he slurred as he hit the floor with a loud thump.

"Ben!" Anna hollered, dropping the staffs and dropping down next to him. She shook his shoulders and peeled one eyelid up. His eyes had rolled back into his head. Something sharp stabbed her in the neck. She slapped at it, began to feel woozy, and dropped onto her back.

• • • •

"NOW...BEFORE SOMEONE sees..." the man growled hastily. Two men grabbed Anna and lifted her off the floor, scurrying out the back door of the hall. They dropped her on the grass as the first man bent down and tugged her breeches down on her right hip. He nodded and let her clothes go. "It's her. Hide her in the dungeon and keep one of these on her..." the man thrust a bracelet into the other man's hand. "If it even seems like she is using her rune casting, slap another one on her."

"Where would I get another one?" the other man retorted.

"In the dungeon there are closets full of them. They have a very limited range of time and then they stop working. Keep a close eye on her."

"What are you going to do?" the other man demanded, grabbing Anna by the arms and hoisting her up over his shoulder.

"I'm going to throw everyone off our trail. Just make sure you take her to the cells I showed you. The cells no one remembers."

• • • •

LIGHTNING SHARP PAINS radiated through Ben's head as he slowly became aware of his surroundings. He gazed around the hall with a frown. There were several people looking distressed, a few looking distraught, and Mikal who looked ready to resort to violence. Something was off. He turned his head and groaned, feeling as if he had been thrown from his horse. Every muscle in his body ached. For some reason, he was looking at the ceiling of the dance hall. Mikal was by his side instantly, grabbing his hand and helping him stand. The room spun and it was all Ben could do to keep from falling back down. Someone had thrust a goblet into his hands and he thankfully downed the water, realizing for the first time how dry his mouth and throat were. The rampaging headache only got worse the longer he stood. Voices were clamoring for his attention, but he couldn't focus his thoughts enough to answer. What the hell had happened?

He tried to remember what he had been doing before he ended up on the floor of the hall. Fuzzy images of Anna walking through the hall of the castle in her workout clothes with two staffs in her hands flitted in and out of his mind. He thought he had been heading down to the hall to have a sparring match with her. The next thing he could remember was waking up and all of these people were milling around in the hall. Mikal returned to his side with a chair and forced him to sit, helping to ease the throb of his head. He knelt down in front of him, grasping his hand, alternately giving comfort and taking it.

"Anna is gone," Mikal spoke in a comforting tone. He watched as Ben cringed at the words, but didn't otherwise move. "Ben...Anna is gone," he repeated.

"Anna..." Ben gasped. He clutched his brothers hand a little tighter. He tried to ignore the pain of his throbbing head and reach out with his power. Nothing. He couldn't feel anything but the rune casters in the room with him. "Anna...was here." He motioned to the room.

"Yes." Mikal coaxed.

"We were...going to spar." Ben inhaled deeply and focused directly on Mikal's face. "I remember something stung me and then...nothing."

"This is very important..." Mikal leaned closer. His words barely discernible over the pounding of his head. "Was Anna anywhere near you when you felt that sting?"

"She was..." Ben leaned his head back and closed his eyes. "She was in front of me...a step or two..."

"Good. That means she didn't attempt to assassinate you."

"What?" Ben's eyes opened wide and he almost tumbled from the chair. "Never..."

"I didn't think it was possible either Ben, but I have to rule it out." Mikal patted his hand and stood. "That means someone knocked you out and stole her away. So instead of looking for a runaway hostage, I am looking for a kidnapper."

"Cael..." Ben stood, tripping over his feet in his haste to get out of the hall. "Jorst...Zura..." A set of small but very strong hands pressed against his thigh and he dropped his tortured gaze to find Juta barring his path. The little dwarf woman was a lot stronger than she looked.

"You sit!" she commanded in her language. "I have already brought Mikal up to date on the situation with those three. Zura and Jorst are still in the wind. Cael is still in the dungeon. It wasn't them."

"Then who..." Ben ran his fingers through his hair and sighed.

"What?" Mikal demanded. "What did you just think of?"

"I announced at the beginning of the week that I am going to marry Anna. It could be anyone."

"You what?" Mikal shouted so loudly that the rest of the people milling around in the hall looked in their direction. "I thought you would be smart enough to wait until the ball at least to make a claim like that. What in Gaia would possess you to make a stupid announcement like that without me here to protect you?"

"There is no need to act as if you are the only one who can fight..." Ben growled. "I did what my heart was telling me to do."

"Enough arguing..." Juta snapped, crossing her arms over her chest. "Mikal, tell Ben what you found out."

"That can wait..." Ben snarled.

"No!" Juta kicked him in the shin and smiled with glee when he rubbed his leg. "I am sick of watching you run around like a preening elf. Listen first..."

"This is probably a conversation that needs to be behind closed doors..." Mikal remarked as he watched eyes turn in their direction. "Come, let's get you to your room. Juta, can you find something for Ben's headache?"

"Maize was in the kitchen a while ago. I'll see if she is still around."

Mikal thanked her as he helped Ben stumble to his room. Once he had him situated behind his desk, he dropped into the chair on the other side and kicked his feet up. Ben only glared at him. A few moments later the door opened and Maize came in. She curtsied and then immediately set her hands along his temples. The soothing relief of her power washed the pulsing headache out of his system, eased the fatigue of his muscles, and helped clear out the cobwebs. It took only a few moments and then she swept out of the room.

Juta opened the door and brought in a tray of tea and some veggies for them to eat since they had missed their evening meal. Ben felt his nerves ready to snap. He just wanted the information Mikal had collected so that he could rush off and rescue Anna. Was that really such a difficult thing to ask? He felt ready to snap when Juta settled into the other chair and then Mikal began.

"I went to Garia, tracing down the rune caster who had been training Princess Alana Sageowl of Garia before she disappeared. Marteen of Garia was a very well-known memory caster. He was sought out by thousands in Garia as well as here in Enderton to block memories, insert skills, or even to just make someone remember happier times. Of course, he was no-where near as good as King Sageowl, but he was definitely good."

"Did you find him?" Juta asked, her cup of tea halfway to her mouth.

"Yes. He wasn't much help though, as he was just a headstone in a burial yard." Mikal rubbed his face and noticed how tense his brother was. "Without this man to trace the missing princess, I was ready to come back here, but then my mind flashed to father's notes. There are thousands of servants and people that run a castle. It is hard to remember every single one of them. It is even harder to vouch for anyone not in your personal service. Something has always been off about father's notes. He listed every single servant in that castle. He had a scribe take down notes of every conversation he had with them. That is when I thought of it."

"What?" Ben demanded, leaning closer.

"There was a servant missing from the list. Princess Alana was five years old when she went missing and her parents were murdered. Of all the servant's father had listed in her personal entourage, he was missing the nursemaid. I can't believe I didn't notice sooner. No royal would ever raise their child without assistance. It just isn't possible."

"Maybe, but..." Ben clasped his hands together and eased back in the chair. "Things work differently in Garia...they could have just used their servants on a rotation..."

"No." Mikal shook his head emphatically. "No, I asked around the village near the castle. Several of the older women agreed that they had employed a nursemaid. Sadly though, none of them remembered her name or what happened to her."

"So, another dead end?" Ben scratched his beard and downed his now cold tea. "We are back to square one then."

"Not so fast..." Mikal popped a few wrinkly grapes in his mouth and smiled. "I said the women in that village didn't remember. That doesn't mean I didn't find what I was looking for."

"Then you found her?"

"I did. It took me a while, but I finally found a young maid that had been groomed to be a lady in waiting for Princess Alana...until she went missing. That young woman not only remembered the nurse maid, but she took me right to her."

"If you tell me that you found her headstone as well..." Ben growled.

"Nope. Princess Alana's nursemaid is none other than Teamalah Forsooth."

"Jumping elfin sparks!" Juta exclaimed as she shot off the chair. "You mean she has been here under our noses this whole time? Princess Alana is actually Anna?" She cackled knowingly and slapped her knee. "I knew that girl had proper breeding in her somewhere. It is the only explanation for her proper manners."

"Anna..." Ben worked the name around his mouth. "Alana..." his forehead creased as he thought about it. "They kept her name similar to ease the transition. Makes sense...but Anna doesn't remember much before her sixth birthday. It can't be her."

"Tell me brother..." Mikal beamed as he popped another grape in his mouth. "Does Anna have a small freckle on her right hip, something that could possibly be interpreted as a star shape?" He watched as Ben's face brightened and then darkened. "I take that as affirmation. So, the woman you are declaring to be a commoner that will become Queen Consort is actually the missing Garian Princess that shall become Queen Alana Braun of Garia and Enderton. Seems to me this makes a simple kidnapping into a bigger more complex enigma."

"Yes...but who knows all of this aside from us and Teamalah and Jasper?"

"That will be the crux of our problem. Someone knows that the missing Garian Princess isn't dead and really isn't missing. If we can figure out who they are, and why they took her, we will have a better idea of where to look. My best guess...the current Garian royalty. They wouldn't want Anna to be found at all. Her claim to the throne, especially now, would be too great. All Anna would need is someone who could prove she was the missing princess, and she would be reinstated to her throne faster than we could blink."

"Then we had better start figuring it out." Ben narrowed his eyes at his two trusted confidants. "I plan to marry Anna regardless of whether she is a princess or not, but I can't do that if I don't know where she is."

Chapter Sixteen

Anna had a splitting headache. She rolled into a ball, tucking her knees to her chest and resting her head on them. Why was her head throbbing so? A sudden cold chill swept through her. Where was she? She peeked around her arms and couldn't see much. It was dark. The feel of the ground under her wasn't pleasant either. It felt slick and wet. Her body ached as she uncurled and tried to stand. The movement made her disoriented and she slipped back down into a ball on the ground.

She closed her eyes. She reached out with her powers and felt nothing. If there was one thing she hated, it was women who acted as if they couldn't care for themselves. She had promised herself that she wouldn't be a simpering fool. Yet, as she lay on this very slimy wet hard floor in the pressing darkness, she began to wonder if she wasn't a useless woman.

She had tried escaping from Ben but ended up giving in when he fell ill. She had been kidnapped by Cael for a whole day and had been unable to rescue herself. And now this...she was taken away again...and she had been powerless to stop it. She really was the most pathetic woman she knew. It would probably be better if she remained lost. Ben could find a stronger woman for sure. A stray tear slipped down her cheek, then another, and another.

She sniffled and heard a scuffling noise to her right. She was stronger than this. She could endure anything. All she had to do was remain alive until she had the chance to escape. She moved to her hands and knees and crawled around until she bumped into a wall. Rune points, she had not cried when she thought she was facing death.

"It's no use..." said a familiar voice. "There is no escaping the dungeon."

"I'm not trying to escape..." Anna grated through her parched throat. "I am checking out the surroundings."

"No need. Might as well curl back up in a ball." The man laughed and his voice suddenly seemed closer. "To think I stole you away in the hopes of forcing you to do something about the blight. Now, here you are. Where you can't do a thing. Just as I am."

"Cael?" she inquired as she continued to feel along the wall and floor. She bumped into something around her head. It was about two feet or so off the floor so she assumed it was her cot or bed. She skimmed around it as she talked. "I'm in the dungeon then?"

"Yep." He laughed again. "You're in the place they put people to forget about them."

"I didn't forget you were down here." Anna finished the circuit of the cell and sighed, crawling up onto her cot. It was a long hard board that had been bolted onto the wall. She sighed as her head throbbed even more. "I mean, you didn't expect the Corrupt King to forgive you for stealing his new possession...did you?"

"I..." he hesitated and then chuckled. "I guess you are right. I was only trying to help the kingdom. To help my family. Now I will rot away here in this dark dank place. I would rather have been run through. Would have been quicker and probably much less painful." He gave a wet sloppy hack.

"You will not rot away here." She wondered how much she should share with him. She wasn't happy about being kidnapped, but she also wasn't angry at him. He didn't harm her...not really. He seemed to have good intentions. "You know he isn't really the Corrupt King, right?"

"Right..." Cael snorted and she heard the sound of rushing liquid. "And I just pissed wine...you must be touched in the head."

"What I mean is...King Braun has already asked me multiple times to aid him with cleaning up the blight. It's just..."

"He would rather tussle with you in the sheets than to actually get down to the pressing issues?"

"NO!" she growled. She crossed her arms over her chest in anger, her cheeks flaming. "Things just kept happening. In fact, I was going to have him take me where this blight started, but then you kidnapped me. I told him to take me just last week but now I am in here...so there," she whined, sticking her tongue out in the dark, knowing he couldn't see it.

There was silence for so long, Anna figured he didn't believe her. She sat crossed legged on the bench, her back and head resting against the wall, her eyes closed since she couldn't see a thing anyways. There seemed to be a few other people down here. She heard random scuffling, rushing liquid, even coughs and gasps. She couldn't believe that Ben would banish this many people down into the darkest part of the dungeon. Then again, she had really only been in his kingdom for a short time. Who knew how many people he had sentenced in that time?

The smell of fresh water assaulted her nose. Her ears picked up the sound of gushing water. She followed the smell to the wall across from her and found a hole where water was pouring out. She opened her mouth and gulped the sweet liquid down. Too soon it dried up and she groaned, making her way back to her cot. Cael shuffled in the cell next to her and tapped on his bench.

"There will be two more of those during the day. Hope you are not hungry, because we only get food when someone remembers us."

"Someone has to remember we are down here..." she insisted. "Otherwise, you wouldn't have gotten water just now."

"Yeah...you don't know much, do you? The dungeons are fed by a water spill off. The spill off gets full and the sluice opens, sending the fresh water into the cells. All cells get water regardless if there is a prisoner in here or not. It is part of the reason why the floor is so slick."

"Well, Cael..." Anna shivered and wrapped her arms around her knees. "I may be ignorant, but I do know that someone will realize I am down here eventually."

"Are you sure he didn't get tired of his new toy and had you brought to the dungeon?" Cael gave another short bark. "I mean, you are a rune caster. You might have been more of a danger than he expected. Speaking of which...can't you just use your power and get yourself out of here?"

"I can't..." Anna felt the metal band around her wrist.

Cael might be closer to the truth than she wanted to believe. The last time she was unable to access her power, Mikal had slapped a metal bracelet on her wrist. She tried to remember what had happened before she blacked out. She had been trying to work off nervous energy. Ben had just announced earlier in the week that he planned to marry her. He had been secluded behind his study door alone with the individuals of his court. She assumed all the socialites that trailed in and out of his study all day were pleading with him to find someone more regal, someone more royal, someone not her. She remembered finally giving up and deciding that she needed to work out her excessive nervousness.

She had changed into her workout clothes and grabbed two staffs out of the hall. She had made her way to Ben's study and tapped on his door. He had smiled, pulling off his outer gear and walking with her to the hall. That's when she remembered him saying something. She had turned and seen him collapsed on the floor. After that, she couldn't remember anything. Either Ben had tired of her and tossed her down here, or someone was attempting a coupe. She prayed it was neither of those. Shuddering from the thought, she tucked her knees tighter to her chest. She could survive for a week. In a week her bracelet would wear out and she could access her power again, right?

"What do you mean you can't?" She heard Cael shuffle closer to her. "You are supposed to be an all-powerful black rune caster! Why can't you?"

"I can't...because someone slapped this rune cursed cuff on me and cut off my power." Anna snorted. "If I can survive a week down here, I can wear the bracelet out and then I can access my power again. Until the bracelet comes off or wears out, I am just an ordinary."

"Great." Cael spat and from the sound, settled onto his own cot. "No chance of redemption then."

"Why not?"

"Your eyes haven't adjusted to the dark yet?" he snapped. "There are two guys watching you like a hawk. I'm guessing they have orders to change out that bracelet of yours when you start showing signs of getting your power back." His voice had dropped dangerously low, but since his cot was just on the other side of the wall, she still heard him.

"Can you make out any details?"

"Just two large shapes. They were larger than you, which is why I am going with male instead of female." Cael's voice dropped a little more. "You seriously can't see anything? I know it is dark, but you should have some sight..."

"To be honest Cael, whatever they knocked me out with has my head pounding so hard, I'm not keeping my eyes open." She peeled one eye open and glanced around. "I can see vague shapes now..."

"Directly across from you and then just down to the left..." he murmured.

Anna scanned the person directly across from her. He was pretty rotund through the middle. His slouched posture made it hard to determine exactly how tall he was. He was fairly pale though, as his skin glowed slightly in the darkness. It still wasn't enough to give her a good idea of who it was. She shifted her sight to the man to the left.

He was also slouched and leaning against the wall. He was just as pale as his counterpart, but where the other was round, this man was slender like a reed. She snapped her eyes closed again and scratched at the band on her wrist. She reached out again with her power, hoping to connect with Ben. The frustration of not being able to access her power was probably the most overwhelming part of this whole situation. If she could just access her power, she would know instantly if Ben was guilty of tossing her down here or if it was someone else. If it was someone else, did Ben know she was right beneath him? Did he have any clue where to look for her? She kept playing with the bracelet.

"Cael..." she whispered so softly she was afraid he wouldn't hear her.

"What?"

"How do the dampening bracelets work?"

"I'm not sure I understand the question. They put them on and it keeps a caster from accessing their power."

"Yes, but how does it work? Does it just shield the person or does it actually cut them off? Is the power of the bracelet based on the number of times a person tries to use their power? If I try accessing my power all day for the next few days, would it burn out faster than if I tried a handful of times over a week?"

"Ah..." Cael sneezed and then sniffled. "I am afraid those are questions only Astrid would know the answers to. And maybe anyone who has access to the library of Rune knowledge. Your guess would be as good as mine at this point princess..."

"I'm not a princess." Anna closed her eyes once more and focused on the bracelet. She sent all her power to it, hoping it would do something. Her head began to pound even harder as a reward for her effort. She sighed in resignation. Best for her to sleep off the headache and maybe when she woke up, she would be clear headed enough to think of a plan.

Chapter Seventeen

"I have sent guards to the surrounding villages of Clodmore, Stagreach, and Roguevalley. I sent them to the small farms between as well. If she is still on this side of the border, we will find her by nightfall." Mikal patted his brother on the shoulder as they settled at the desk in the study. Mikal was tugging on the cord around his neck, fingering the small carved pig that Anna had given to him as a child. He noticed Ben was gazing at the small carved monkey on his bookshelf. "If she is in the edge villages and farms or across the border, it will be a few days."

"Your highness!" Juta interrupted, opening the door and strolling in without permission. Ben's eyes instantly snapped up to her hopefully. "I have interviewed all of the maids and most of the servants. None have seen her since she went to fetch you for her exercise. Shall I begin investigating the guests?" she asked with an evil grin. Her fingers rubbed back and forth as she waited for an answer.

"No Juta." Ben rubbed his face with frustration. Anna had been gone for almost a whole day at this point. He worried something worse had happened to her. "I think maybe we all three need to interview our guests. That way we don't miss a single thing."

"Are you prepared to fully interrogate them?" Mikal inquired, propping his feet up on the desk. "Use your power to get them to answer?"

"You know what you are asking me..." Ben growled in annoyance. He heaved a heavy sigh and rested his arms on his desk. "I will do what I must to get answers. If that means I have to use my power to persuade them, I certainly will."

"As long as we are all on the same page." Mikal popped up out of the chair and strode to the door with a smile on his face. "Shall we start with the princess or her underlings?"

"Might as well work our way down from the top..." As he waited for Mikal to return, a woman stepped into the study with a tray of tea and pastries. Ben glanced at Juta who gave him a slight nod. He waved the maid off and she curtsied before leaving the room just as Mikal returned with their guest. Juta had grabbed a chair from the dining room and situated herself as comfortably as she could. "Princess Elena..." Ben paused, taking a sip of his tea as he studied the princess.

Princess Elena was dressed slightly more appropriately today than she had when she arrived. Her dress was styled in the Garian fashion in a lovely pale sage color. He noticed her makeup and hair were still styled lavishly and the matching jewels at her neck were gaudy. He tried to look past the six inches of makeup to the woman underneath. He tried to focus specifically on her as a person and not what she entailed. More importantly, he tried to reach out with his power without her realizing he was. He knew that she was a red rune caster. He also knew that she was a very weak one. He watched as her eyes traveled all over his body. Good. If she was distracted enough by him and his power, she wouldn't notice as he pushed for answers.

"Princess Elena...a very important member of my castle has disappeared. I was wondering if you knew anything that might help us find her."

"Oh my, Bennie..." she gasped, her manicured hand flashing up to her mouth in shock. "I will do whatever it takes in order to help you and your staff, Your Highness!"

"Where were you yesterday evening?" Ben pushed a little harder with his telepathy and watched as she shuffled slightly in her chair, her hand waving back and forth in front of her face.

"Uh...well...I am not sure what time you mean, but I had dinner with my ladies and then I retired for the evening to my chambers. We had been visiting Roguevalley which is so far away and I was exhausted."

"Tell us...what do you know about the missing Garian princess." Mikal watched as her left eyebrow quirked and then her eyes narrowed as she turned her gaze to him.

"I am not missing." Her mouth was pressed firmly together as she glared at him. "If you are insinuating that my family..."

"I'm not insinuating anything." Mikal crossed his arms over his chest and tilted his head. "Sageowl's were the ruling family in Garia for centuries and now, we have the Mawhorter's on the throne. What happened to the former princess?"

"The Sageowl's were unfit to rule..." Elena remarked, crossing her arms over her chest. She turned her gaze back to Ben, her eyes flashing red. The parchments on his desk began to smolder lightly. "I suggest that this horrid insinuation be dropped now."

"Or?" Juta replied with a frown. "Do you plan to burn down our castle?" When the woman only glanced in her direction Juta growled and switched to the common tongue. "Does that mean you plan to burn down our castle?"

"I don't talk with servants..." Elena remarked, tipping her head back. "The Mawhorter's are the true lineage to the Garian throne. As such, you are commanded to wed me or lose your claim to the dwarven mountains. Since you made it so publicly clear that you chose another woman for your wife, I sent notice to my parents just yester eve that you will forfeit the mountains. Now, is there anything else you wish to discuss?"

"Dwarves are not owned, you spindly elfin twat. That includes our mountains..." Juta sniffed, crossing her arms angrily and glancing away from her.

"Where is Anna?" Ben sighed, easing back in his seat. In hindsight, making his proclamation to marry Anna public knowledge was probably the worst thing he could have done.

"Anna?" Elena raised a brow and smiled. "Your low born unintelligent bride to be that cost you the mountains has come up missing?" She laughed, tossing back her head, her make-up cracking lightly along her eyes and mouth. "Oh...this is too good. Did the commoner run off, afraid of the responsibilities, frightened of the Corrupt King?"

"Remove her from my sight..." Ben growled in disgust, flicking his hand toward her. Mikal moved quickly around the desk but not fast enough. Elena jumped from the chair and strode to the door, still tittering with laughter. Mikal stepped into the hall and returned a few moments later with the prime minister of Garia. He balanced himself on the edge of the chair the princess had just vacated. Just as with the princess, he was dressed in more sensible clothing today, albeit still very expensive. His black leather breaches were tailored expertly around his legs and waist. His tunic was made of silk and of the brightest shade of chartreuse. He had on a pair of vivid purple leather boots with three-inch heels. Ben tried not to show how much his sense were offended. The man's hair was curled and powdered. Ben inhaled deeply, trying to remain calm. "Prime Minister Jesper Bulgar...a very important member of my castle has disappeared."

"Oh no..." Jesper said without a hint of emotion. Ben pushed with his mental power and watched as the man's ruddy complexion seemed to go a little sallow. He instantly crossed his legs and coughed. "I hope everything works out eventually."

"Care to tell me where you were last evening?"

"Uh, I was..." Jesper adjusted in the chair and darted his gaze between the brothers. "I uh...oh dear...what was the question again?"

"What were you doing last evening?" Mikal asked, bending and propping his hands on the desk to glare at the minister. "Just before the evening meal...where were you?"

"Oh...uh..." he tapped his finger against his lip and sighed. "Let me think."

Ben watched in fascination as the man bolted from the chair and rushed out into the hall like a spry teenager and not the sixty-year-old man he knew him to be. Mikal flew around the desk but was knocked back by a force of wind so strong, it slammed the door of the study open. Juta was the next one out the door. Ben followed behind her, sure they wouldn't catch him. The man was a hidden yellow rune caster. He could force everyone back with just a gust of wind. Sounds of chaos flooded the halls as they searched for the missing minister. Ben eventually held up his hand and leaned against the wall.

"We are never going to catch him. The other two men..."

"They have been missing since last night," Mikal confirmed. "The two ladies in waiting are still here if you want to interrogate them."

"No. If they are sitting tight, then they were not in on this plot." Ben rubbed his face and moved back to his study. "If the Prime

Minister knows that Anna is Alana, that means the Mawhorter's surely know it as well. Did you get the same feel from Elena?"

"She knows that there is another princess that can refute her claim." Mikal dropped back into the chair with a sigh.

"That's what I am thinking. We have three men who kidnapped her and know that Anna is the true Garian princess."

"They are here somewhere..." Juta exclaimed as she rushed inside the study. Her eyes were twinkling. "I followed that foul beastie's trail. He double-backed at the forest. He's here in this castle somewhere!"

"Mikal..." Ben urged. He rose from his chair and they all rushed into the hallway.

"Already there, brother! Guards...search the castle. The Prime Minister must be apprehended. He is a yellow caster, approach him with extreme caution. Astrid!"

"Mikal..." she replied, jogging up by him.

"You are the only yellow rune caster in the castle. Can you search him out with your power like Anna does with me?" Ben demanded.

"I'm not sure. I haven't used my power that way..." Astrid's eyes flashed yellow and began glowing. Her brow wrinkled as Ben, Juta and Mikal waited, holding their breath. "I can feel him...but I can't..." Astrid began panting as she pushed her power harder. She swayed and began to fall when Mikal caught her.

"Don't push yourself. If you can't find him..." Mikal warned.

"He's here somewhere. It's all I can get." Astrid gasped as they all turned and started to rush room to room in search of him. "Wait..." she called, with a wince. "Anna is here..."

"What?" They all exclaimed as she shut her power off and bent over, putting her hands on her knees.

"Anna is here in the castle? Ben demanded. He reached out with his own power, seeking her black rune power, but he couldn't feel anything.

"Where child?" Juta begged.

"It is...very faint...an impression...I think...she's here. I see...a shadow."

"Where?" Ben realized he was yelling at the top of his lungs and inhaled deeply. He stepped forward, placed a calming hand on her shoulder, and tried again. "I'm sorry Astrid, where are they? Can you see a location, anything to narrow down the search?"

"The best I...they are here. It's like..." Astrid stood up and looked around. "It's almost as if...we are on top of them. That's the best I can do." Astrid accepted parchments from a guard who rushed into the hallway. She glanced at the missive and exhaled deeply. "She is nowhere in the area farms or villages. My guards are riding on to the border towns and then across the border into Garia."

"We just have to keep searching. I'll take the hidden places..." Mikal said.

"Wait!" Juta jumped up and down a couple of times as she stared at the floor. "Right below us. We are on top of them. They are in the dungeon...the dark one..."

"What better place for them to hide her than the place we put people to forget about them." Ben nodded and started toward the dungeons at a run.

It seemed as if it took ten years for them to run through the hallways and get to the dungeons and then another ten years to finally make it to the dark part. Ben had grabbed a torch on his way down one of the dungeon halls. He had very few people in this part of the dungeon as he preferred to be a generous king instead of the corrupt king. He had four men that he had put down here for being serial murderers. He had one serial rapist and he had Cael whose biggest crime was stealing Anna from him. He knew he couldn't leave Cael down here. He needed to have him removed and given community service of some sort, but things had spiraled out of his control. He rounded the corner of the cells and felt his heart plummet into his stomach. Fear and dread both washed through him. The prisoners were all released, there were five dampening bracelets strewn across the floor, and Cael was lying on his face in the middle of them. He stalked forward and dropped to his knees next to Cael, feeling for a pulse.

"He's alive...but barely." Ben spat. "We need Maize." He watched as Juta turned deftly on her heels and sprinted back out of the dungeons. "Cael..." Ben said as he turned him over and patted his cheek.

"N-n-no!" Cael cried, reaching out. He caught the king's tunic in his hand and then his eyes shot open. He immediately dropped his hand and turned his head away from him. "She's gone...I tried...to save her, but..."

"Best save your strength. I sent for Maize to come and heal you."

"He took..." Cael coughed and blood covered his lower lip. "Bulgar..."

"We know."

Four guards and Maize came around the corner. She instantly dropped to her knees and her eyes began glowing blue. Cael coughed again and groaned. Ben stood and paced around the area. Mikal was doing the same. Astrid joined them, her power glowing in her eyes.

"It appears they knew about the dampening bracelets and took as many as they could to keep her off our radar." Ben stated as he pointed to the bracelets.

"Not enough your highness." Astrid smiled and winked. "I can still sense a shadow near a yellow glow. They are heading northwest...towards the black forest."

"Why the black forest?" Mikal glanced over as Cael groaned once more and sat up. "That doesn't make sense."

"It does, your highness..." Cael scooted a few feet to the wall and leaned against it, pushing to his feet. The guards rushed to his side and caught his arms.

"Leave him..." Ben growled. "Speak Cael. What do you know?"

"Bulgar wants her to do what I wanted her to do. He said she had to heal the forest." Cael pushed his hair out of his face and groaned, nodding to Maize as she caught his arm. "He released all of us with the hopes we would be his guard as he smuggled her out of here. I fought to free her."

"Does everyone think that I am incompetent?" Ben shook his head and held up his hand. "Don't answer that. We know exactly where he is taking her. We need to make a plan."

"What about him?" Mikal asked as he motioned to Cael.

"While I don't appreciate the kidnapping of my future wife," Ben coughed and glared at him. "I am pretty sure he did try to rescue her. Anna is getting good at her self-defense training but not good enough to take on all the men down here. Most of this struggle was probably from Cael."

"Yes, your highness." Cael chuckled and stepped forward. "But you will be happy to know she took down his two lackies before Jesper himself grabbed her."

"Cael, I absolve you of your crime. You are free to go with my thanks for trying to save Anna."

"If I may, I want to help you get her...you are going to need more hands..."

Ben stood looking deep into Cael's eyes without saying a word. Mikal moved to say something but then paused as he too looked at him.

"Look, I know I was wrong in kidnapping her. I only wanted her to heal the forest. My intention was never to harm her. My bloody farm borders that damn forest. I have as much at stake in getting her back safe as you all."

"Very well..." Mikal turned to Maize and gave her a soft smile. "Maize darling, are you up for a little riding? I have a feeling we will need your services..."

"Yes, your highness..." Maize returned the smile and dipped a curtsy. "Cael isn't fully healed, but I need a few moments rest and I will finish before we mount up."

"Juta," Ben turned and found the little dwarven woman bouncing up and down on her toes. "Let's get a riding party together and meet in my chambers to discuss a plan. These damn Garian's have been two steps ahead of us this whole time. I am not letting her slip out of my fingers yet again."

"Yes...right away!"

"Mikal, assemble a crew of those we trust."

"Already on it..."

"Astrid..."

"This is a new way of using my power, your highness." Astrid apologized, but nodded her head and smiled. "But I am doing my best to keep a general map of where they are."

"Thank you, Astrid, but I was going to have you get some rest and then send a message to our people in Garia to prepare." Ben smiled softly at her as she appeared ready to collapse.

"I will not rest until she is back safe and sound. Forgive me for my frankness, but she is good for you...and the kingdom. Besides...I already told our people in Garia to prepare a few weeks ago."

"Very well, I can't force you to rest. Just try not to burn yourself out." He watched as she smiled and nodded. "Let's get a plan together. Come Cael, we could use another person to help us brainstorm."

Chapter Eighteen

Anna groaned deep in her throat as she slowly came to. Goddess damn the Rune Points, she was on a horse, hanging like a sack of flour again, with her ribs cracking against the pommel. Her feet were unbound, but her hands had been cuffed somehow. She blinked the blurriness from her vision and tried to focus on her cuffs. The devious captor had used three dampening bracelets and concocted a crude sort of manacle around her wrists. She might have been able to wear out one bracelet but she was sure she wouldn't be able to wear out three of them. She tried to twist and look at who held her, but the pain lancing through her head and side was too much to bear. Better to just lie here until they came to a stop.

She studied the area and the ground as the horse galloped along. The leaves of the plants were all withered and black. The bushes were black sticks with no leaves, and the ground held no grass. She was being hauled into the black forest. She was relieved at first that she would be able to help heal the land, but then she realized she was being held captive. This couldn't be a good thing. She focused on the bracelets again and pushed with all her power. She wasn't going down without a fight. She couldn't.

"Even you are not powerful enough to break three of those..." the childish male voice said. "I'll take them off soon enough. I just need to make sure we are in the correct spot."

"What do you want from me?" Anna growled. "I mean, seriously? What have I done now?"

"You are going to cure this blight. If you can cure it where it started, the healing will ripple across the land. If I can bring proof that you cured this blight and made the land fertile again, my King will murder Braun and unite the kingdoms in the way they should be."

"Why would I help you?" Anna laughed hysterically. "Why do men always think they have to kidnap people and force them to do their will?"

"Would you have done it if we had asked politely?" the man whined.

"Goddess no. Why would I want anyone to be murdered, let alone Braun? Where do the Garian royalty get off thinking they are better than Braun?"

"They are the true descendants of the original Corrupt King. They will restore order to our divided kingdom."

"For the love of all that is holy…" Anna rubbed her eyes and sighed heavily. How the Garian's could think they were the true descendants of the original corrupt king she would never know. The only people who would be able claim that would be Ben as he has the same power. The horse took a turn and she grunted as the pommel dug into her ribs again. The man yanked back on the reins and jumped from the saddle the moment the horse stopped. She didn't fight him as he yanked her down and settled her on her feet. Anna turned in a circle, looking at the devastation that Ben had caused.

The trees had shriveled and shrunk into black and gray shells of their former beauty. There was no grass, only mud and dirt beneath her feet. The forest was deathly silent as no animals moved or birds flew through here. She reached out and caught her captor's arm but not for emotional support. She felt as if she was going to fall flat on her face from the oppressive feel of the forest. She released his arms as soon as she felt steady, turning full circle to look directly at her captor. Go figure, it was the bulbous prime minister. "You'll have to remove these if you want me to do anything."

"I'm quicker and stronger than I look..." he warned as he pressed on the bracelets and they fell off. "I strongly suggest you don't do anything against us."

At his words, two other men melted from the shadows, their horses trailing behind them. She exhaled and swiped her hair from her face. Right, this was tall and skinny and short and fat from the dungeon. She was pleasantly happy to see tall and skinny kept adjusting his trousers. Her knee to the groin had left a lasting impression to him at least. She sank to her knees and buried her hands into the ground. Reaching out with her power, she probed the magical aura of the forest. The power felt familiar of course, since it was Ben's power who caused it, but she hadn't been prepared for the emotional attack. If she hadn't been on her knees to begin with, she would have fallen down.

Tears streamed down her face, crippling sorrow filled her chest, and anger burned in her mind. She pulled a small ball of her black power and pushed it into the ground. She felt more than saw her power being swallowed up. She pulled more power and shoved. This was swallowed up as well, but there were no visible signs of change on the earth beneath her hands. Anna inhaled deeply and wished she knew more about rune casting. She was so out of her league on this. If Ben were here, he could probably coach her in the right direction at least. She narrowed her eyes over at the prime minister and saw that he had a fairly large yellow orb inside his chest.

"You are a rune caster?" she tossed at him.

"Of course..." he raised his nose a little further in the air and sniffed in disgust at her question. "What type of true Garian wouldn't be?"

"You want me to heal the land...you have any idea how I am supposed to do that?" Anna rolled her eyes at his show of snobbery. "Everyone keeps telling me I can heal what happened here, but no one seems to know how I am supposed to do it."

"You mean you can't?" he asked with horror on his face.

"I grew up here in Enderton. I may have rune power, but I never learned how to use it." Anna pulled her hands out of the soil and wiped them on her trousers. "If you want to give me an idea of how to do it, I will be happy to heal the land."

"Well, I don't know how. I just assumed a black rune caster would automatically know how." He crossed his arms primly over his chest and then glared at her. She was just reaching out with her power to try and knock the three men out when a fleshy arm wrapped around her body, pulling her against a male chest. The improvised manacle was slapped back over her wrist and she was released to stumble forward, falling back to her knees. "If you behave yourself, I'll let you sit astride the horse this time."

"How about you leave me here. I am no good to you."

"No, I am sure King Mawhorter has other things he can use you for." He gave her a smug sneer as he shoved her onto his horse. "Besides, I can't let the true Garian Princess run off again. You may have survived your assassination as a child, but I won't make that mistake twice."

What in Gaia was wrong with this man? Anna sat stiffly in the saddle as he whipped the horse into a gallop towards Garia. There was no way he thought she was the missing Garian Princess, right? Holy Goddess, if that is what he thought, what did they have planned for her?

• • • •

BEN TRIED HARD NOT to spur his horse to go faster. He didn't want to kill the poor beast. They sped through the forest as fast as he felt safe given the late evening sun was starting to set. Mikal, Astrid, Juta, Cael and Maize were all plunging forward at the same speed. Before he left, he had given strict orders that the Garian princess and the remaining delegation needed to vacate the castle. He also gave his guard orders to keep vigilant in case of attack and that no one was allowed into their castle. He noticed the familiar signs that they were nearing the area where he first lost control of his power. He slowed his horse and studied the area as it came into view.

They were not here, but he could clearly see that they had been. He dropped down from the saddle and glanced at the ground. There were three distinct sets of horse prints. They came from three different directions, then merged and went in the direction of the Border Towns. He noticed there were two large furrows in the ground. He walked over to them and studied them as Astrid and Mikal caught up to him. Astrid tilted her head and frowned.

"She tried to do something..." Astrid knelt down and hovered her hand over the furrows in the ground. "There are residual traces of her power here."

"Is there a lot?" Ben asked, hoping that Bulgar hadn't attempted to drain her power into the ground. "Did they drain her?"

"It isn't a lot...not anywhere the size of what she is capable of." Astrid shook her head and sighed. "What are they doing? They kidnap her, hide her in the dungeon, then drag her here, force her to do something, and then take off again."

"I have a feeling my long-term plan of hiding rune casters in Garia as a battle force is going to be very prudent planning on my part."

"You think..." Mikal glanced at Juta as she joined them. "You think they want to take Enderton?"

"Why else would they bring her here?" Ben inquired as he motioned around at the forest. "The only reason to bring her here would be to heal the forest. They could have gone directly to Garia."

"These..." Juta motioned in the direction of Garia, then spat on the ground in disgust. "These impostor royals think they can rule everyone. I've had reports from the mountains they have made several attempts to over run our home."

"Then..." Mikal scratched his head and looked between the two as he thought hard. "They brought her here to heal the land so they could...do what? I just don't follow the process. They could invade our land anytime. They didn't need to try healing the land first."

"My guess is they want to know the land can be healed before they invade. What's the point of taking our lands by force if all they have to do is wait for us to starve?" Ben grabbed the reins of his horse and narrowed his gaze on the ground where the three sets of horse prints merged. "Astrid...if there is any way to get word to our people on the borders...tell them to get a group together of at least twenty strong soldiers and be ready. If I have to storm the castle to bring her back, I will."

"That's an act of war..." Juta warned with a cheesy smile as her horse easily caught up to him.

"If they want to wage war on me, so be it. I'll bring the war to them."

Ben and Mikal strategized the many ways they could see this working out as they rode hard for the border towns. Juta and Astrid provided their own feedback as they trailed behind. As they entered one of the more popular border towns, Ben noticed several of his guard in the village. Astrid and Mikal both disappeared to the rookery so they could send birds and collect any messages that had come in. Easing his horse up next to one of his guards, he watched the people milling about in the town square.

"Why are you here?" Ben asked as quietly and casually as possible. "I thought I left strict orders to guard the castle and not let anyone inside."

"You did, your highness..." the guard said, turning his head as he watched a couple stroll by. They tipped their heads to him and he returned the gesture with a smile. "If what we feared has come to pass, most of us would rather be fighting for our land than watching that pile of rocks. There is a large guard left at the castle...mostly those who are older or who have families to worry about, but the rest of us came to back up our secret forces."

"I could have you thrown in the dungeon for insubordination."

"As far as I am concerned, Your Highness, it would be well worth it. I'd rather you have a show of too much force, than not enough." The guard turned and smiled at Ben. "Besides, I want the little lady back as much as you. We were all tired of playing the Corrupt King ruse. We think it is time we toss that aside and start living as we should."

"How is that then?" Ben asked with a large grin himself.

"Happy and free."

"Very well." Ben watched another couple stroll by that winked at him before dropping their gaze to the ground and looking depressed. "Get me twenty of your men. I've got twenty rune casters coming. We need a place to strategize."

"The Crockery Pub..." he offered.

"Nightfall."

"Yes, Your Highness." The guard chuckled as the king disappeared slowly from sight.

Chapter Nineteen

Juta sat on her mini-pony and watched as Mikal and Ben finalized plans with their team. She couldn't wait for the battle to start. She already had visions of pushing her way through to the castle and rescuing King and Queen Mawhorter from certain death so she could deliver the death blow herself. She distinctly heard Ben say something about no killing and slumped in the saddle, shooting him a glare that would make an elf wither and die. How did that boy think he was going to win a war if he couldn't kill a few of the innocents to get to the rotten core? She pulled her dagger out of her boot sheath and flicked it under her nails as she waited.

The Mawhorter's had dealt too much death and injury to her people over the last twenty years. She wouldn't sit on her horse and play nicely. She couldn't. She had to make sure her people were safe and the only way she knew how to do that was to make this stubborn fool Ben unite the kingdoms under his rule. She hadn't become his mother's seamstress just because she liked fashion. Oh no, far from it. Juta sniffed when Ben remarked once more about not killing and then looked pointedly at her. She simply tossed her thick long braid over her shoulder and pointedly continues to clean her nails with her knife.

Juta had been sent to the Braun's as an apprentice seamstress. The dwarven nation had a prophecy about a young girl who would free their people from the human's tyranny and enslavement. That prophecy had spoken of rune caster's, one white and one black. She had begun fostering Ben as a child. When his mother had passed away, she worked even harder to instill her beliefs in him. He saw her as a mother figure. It was enough for her to know that he would always do the right thing. He would see to it that her people were free to roam the mountains and live where they wanted. He would see to it that the enslavement of her people on the Garian side would come to an end. She knew that if she didn't get Princess Alana back to him, this whole plan would fall apart fast.

She heard the sound of the horses slowly moving out and she sheathed her knife. She was ready for anything. She made sure her horse was near his as the non-fatal war party moved forward. She wanted to slap the boy on the head twice for his stupidity. The Mawhorter's would only laugh when they rode up with twenty guards. They would laugh harder when Ben told them they would attack if they didn't release Anna. At least Ben had been smart enough to get Mikal to call animals along the way. They now had a small non-human force that could also be deployed. Juta smiled a very lethal smile as they pulled up in front of the castle a few hours later. Two days of camping on this side of the border had made her cranky and ready for action. There was no way she was going to miss out on anything. She maneuvered her horse closer to Ben's.

• • • •

"HALT!" A WOMAN YELLED from atop the castle battlements. "State your business!"

"King Ben Braun of Enderton!" Ben shouted as he spurred his horse just a touch closer to show he was the one talking. "I have come to demand you release Anna Forsooth, future Queen Consort of Enderton, immediately. Failure to do so will constitute an act of war."

"There is no one in this castle under the name of Anna Forsooth!" the guard replied back.

"You have one hour to produce her unharmed or I will charge this castle!" Ben watched the flurry of activity behind the guard. They knew exactly who he was talking about. They wouldn't be sending people scurrying to the King otherwise.

"I told you already! There is no one here by that name." The guard leaned forward and glanced down the row of people lined up behind the attacking King. "Are you serious in thinking you can besiege our castle with twenty men?"

Ben didn't respond, merely sat as patiently as he could upon his horse. At the half hour, he motioned behind him. All of his crew advanced another hundred feet toward the castle. There was more excited activity in the guard tower at their approach. He halted his men and pulled on his ear to signal his other plan. The two riders on either end of his party broke from the ranks, turned and raced their horses back behind the Enderton guards.

He glanced up at the sky and smiled as three of his hidden rune casters worked their casting. The skies began to darken, the rumble of thunder rose in the background, and drops of rain began to fall. The enemy guards were being pelted with shards of ice as the temperature dropped a few degrees. A blue caster was pulling in the rain and ice and a yellow caster whipped up the wind. The wind lashed against the castle hard enough to make it creak and groan.

The enemy guards struggled to hold their footing against the barrage. Several fell to the winds and were blown back against the castle walls. The castle shook as his hidden green rune caster pulled on the earth. He patted his horse on the neck as it nickered in fear. The horse snorted and pawed at the ground as vines began to sprout around the feet of the Garian guards. They twisted and rose moving like snakes as they found the path of least resistance to the castle walls. The vines began to sprout blood red roses as they climbed and pushed against the wall causing a scraping noise as the mortar between the stones crumbled and the stones rubbed against each other.

Ben glanced over at Mikal and nodded as Mikal's eyes glowed orange. Animals of all types began to advance behind the guards. A bear roared at a Garian guard who shrieked when he caught sight of the bear out of the corner of his eye. He turned and stabbed at the animal with his sword. The bear swatted with a massive paw, knocking the sword from the frightened guard's hand. The bear stood on his hind legs and roared once again. The guard bolted out of position, screaming back into the castle.

Mikal's eyes flashed darker orange as birds shrieked overhead and began circling and diving at the guards in front of them. Talons gouged a few deep slashes on cheeks and arms sending a few more guards fleeing into the castle. He watched as a couple of rams headbutted two guards who attempted to flee away into the gardens on the right of the castle. Ben called Mikal's attention to the rams and watched as they successfully pulled the random fleeing guards back to the group.

A bloated red-faced man with long gray hair poked his face out the window of the guard tower. Ben was pretty sure he saw a crown on the man's head. It had now been almost forty-five minutes. He started to raise his hand to advance his team closer when the bloated red-faced man appeared on the battlements.

King Mawhorter used to be a medium height, trim gentleman with blonde hair, brown eyes, tan skin and a deep booming voice. The man standing on the battlements was nothing like the man Ben used to know. His blonde hair had turned to a dove gray. His trim body was now obese and bursting the seams of his clothing. His booming voice was now more like the patter of rain as he wheezed with each word. Even his tan skin was now pasty white with red blotches.

Ben nudged his horse in the side and moved closer to hear what the king was saying. It appeared as if he wasn't saying much of anything but just waving his arms around in the air and gasping every few seconds. Angry that he was being delayed, Ben motioned to his team and waited as they advanced another hundred feet. The brown eyes widened, the hands became more frantic in their waving and the King leaned over the battlements.

"Wait!" King Mawhorter shouted. "Wait...we have no clue who Anna Forsooth is! What you're doing is an act of war."

"You are damned right it is!" Ben hollered back. "Release the future Queen Consort of Enderton now or I will raze your castle in the blink of an eye!"

"You wouldn't dare...not if you think she is in here!"

Damn...that was the one thing he was hoping the king wouldn't think of. Ben shifted in his saddle and laughed wildly. "Haven't you heard Mawhorter? I am the Corrupt King. I dare to do a lot of things. I'd rather her die than for you to have your hands on her."

"Now look here Braun..." the king's red face grew a darker shade of red, bordering on purple. He raised his arms and was just getting ready to yell some more when the slimy Prime Minister slithered up next to him. They talked in quiet voices before Mawhorter turned back. Guards flooded out of the gate to the castle and stood at attention in front of Ben's guard. Ben turned his gaze back up to the fake king. Rage filled Mawhorter from head to toe. "You dare make demands of me? I am the true king of this land! I am the direct descendant of our former patriarchy! If anyone shall make demands, it is I. I demand you to leave my sight or I will destroy your pathetic guard."

"You'll hand Anna over!"

"NO!"

There it was. The moment Ben was waiting for. It was the most direct confession that Anna was somewhere inside this castle that he could hope for. That direct refusal to hand her over along with the appearance of her kidnapper to begin with, made Ben's blood begin to boil. With a hungry gleam in his eye, he pulled the sword from his scabbard and yelled to his guard. They spurred their horses forward and all began yelling and screaming as they pressed the attack against the fifty guards that had flooded out of the castle. Mikal spurred the animals forward helping them corral the extra force.

Ben shouted for restraint as he pushed through the throng, blocking swords and knives as they cleared more distance. Juta was by his side and while she was leaving her mark on her attackers, she wasn't killing them. He thanked the Goddess she was showing restraint. He had a feeling that if Juta came across any of the Mawhorter's, it would be a very different story. Within an hour, the whole contingent of fifty guards were surrounded by his twenty men and the animals Mikal had under command. He raised his sword in salute to the king on the wall.

"Check, your highness!" Ben snarled. "I'll give you one more chance." The rain pelted down harder and the sky became slightly darker at his words. "Hand over Anna Forsooth now or I will take your castle by force."

Mawhorter hooted with laughter as more guards flooded from the building to surround them. "Did you seriously think that was all of my guards? You must think me a joke. I will never hand over Alana. I will never let you take my crown! I will take your kingdom.

Play nice little boy and I might even let you live in the dungeon with the forgotten princess."

Ben nodded at Mikal. Mawhorter had just confirmed that he knew the true identity of Anna. Mikal called up his power, his eyes flashed orange once more. The animals advanced, pushing the enemy guards into a tight circle. Ben sat as calmly on his horse as possible and focused on his own rune power. He focused on the guard walls and the guard towers. His eyes flashed white and slowly the rocks began to crumble and flake. The metal began to rust and bend. He heard people inside as they started to scream in horror.

The imposter king himself screamed like a woman as he scrambled off the wall. The lesser-known side, the passive trait of Ben's power, was destruction. He hated using it, but it was the only way he knew to force the other king down from the battlements. Ben turned his white flashing eyes and sought out Juta and Cael. Juta nodded, laughed delightedly, then turned her mini-pony and shoved through the crowd of guards. Still, she didn't kill any innocent people, only maiming and hurting as she went. He let out a pent-up breath at that. He wasn't sure how long he could keep her from murdering someone. Cael wouldn't be able to hold her back if the dwarven woman decided she was getting rid of someone. Cael nodded to him, pushed his way through the throng of guards and followed Juta.

For a brief moment, Ben allowed the anger and disappointment to wash over him as the front wall of the guard tower and battlements became rubble. He was angry that he had probably hurt several people with that show of power. He was angry because the Mawhorter's thought they were in control of everyone. More importantly, he was disappointed that he wouldn't be the one to rescue Anna. He wanted to scoop her out of whatever prison cell they had shoved her into. He wanted to check every inch of her skin to make sure she wasn't harmed. He wanted to fold her up into his embrace and inhale the scent of her hair.

Frustration grew in his mind as he opened his eyes and watched as the wannabe king attempted to run into the castle grounds for cover. The man looked like a drunk elephant as he swung from side to side. Cael circled around as he caught sight of the man. Juta was already gone in pursuit of her own mission. Using his horse, Cael turned the wannabe king back towards the waiting melee in front of the castle. With a few well-placed prods, he maneuvered him over to Ben.

• • • •

"JUTA…" CAEL CALLED as they ran into the castle foyer. The dwarven woman had her knives out and twirling in her hands as she rushed towards the staircase.

"Check the dungeons…" Juta hollered over her shoulder.

She didn't dare slow down. She was going to get a Mawhorter in her clutches if it was the last thing she did today. If she had to make a wild guess, she would figure the Queen and the Princess would be taking refuge in their bedrooms. She threw open all the doors along one hall as she went. Juta narrowed her gaze as she came up empty handed, even of general servants.

It seemed as if they had known about the attack ahead of time. Juta turned and rushed down another hall, pausing at what was obviously the Princess's room. The décor was all pink's and red, there was lavish gilt on every surface, jewels lined the edges of most of the furniture, and even the bed clothes were made of the most expensive silks. She shook her head as she checked under the bed, in the wardrobe, in the private dressing chamber. When she came up empty handed, Juta growled and turned to the other rooms.

This hall was completely empty of servants as well. She darted back across the hall and past the foyer into the east wing. All the rooms on the first hall were empty and when she finally reached the King's quarters, she was ready to stab someone. This room was just as lavish as the Princess's quarters. The room had been done up in a theme of red from the drapes on the walls to the pillows on the beds. Juta glanced through the wardrobes, under the bed and again in each of the private dressing chambers, but the Queen wasn't here either. Back down to the main floor, Juta went through all of the public rooms and found no one except a handful of servants. She issued orders to the servants that they move to the main hall to await further instruction. This was not working out to be a good day. Juta moved to the main foyer to wait for Cael.

· · · ·

CAEL WATCHED JUTA RUN up the stairs and shuddered to think what she would do to the Mawhorter's if she caught them. She was a dwarven woman on a mission and he pitied the person who got in her way. He found the staircase that led down to the dungeons. He moved carefully down, holding a torch above his head as he went. The staircase was wickedly curved and dangerously worn. A few of the stairs were crumbled completely. He shuddered to think what would happen if he wasn't paying attention.

Reaching the bottom, he went cell by cell, looking for Anna or any clue where she was. Each of the cells were empty, closed and locked. They were about as delightful as the one he had inhabited for a week. When he got to the end, he turned, looking for other hidden passages or rooms, but he saw none. Save for the guard room at the end and the one long row of cells, this was it. He turned and looked back, noticing for the first time that one of the cell doors was open. He glanced inside and let out a sigh.

Anna had been in here. The wall showed signs of recent scraping as if she had been pushing something hard against it. Pieces of rocks littered the ground below it. She was here somewhere. He just had to find her. He rushed back up the stairs and joined Juta. Both held their hands out to show they had found nothing. Juta and Cale sighed heavily in frustration.

"Nothing," Juta remarked morosely.

"Same, only Anna is here somewhere. She had been in a cell. There are signs of recent scraping against one of the rock walls. There are chips of rock on the ground..." Cael rubbed his face and glanced around. For as large as the battlements and castle walls were, the Garian castle was tiny compared to the one in Enderton. "Where do you think they moved her?"

"The battlements?" Juta asked, glancing up at the battlement walls. She turned her gaze over to Cael and they both rushed to the staircase. "Go right, I'll take left..." she hollered.

• • • •

"THIS IS COMPLETELY ridiculous..." Mawhorter whined from behind the reserve guards that had poured out. "You can't possibly take over my whole castle with just twenty men."

Ben nodded to Mikal. While his brother's eyes flashed orange once more, Ben only watched as the new set of fifty guards pressed forward. His twenty men were currently holding the first set down on their knees. A few men would rise and try to break through the circle, but his men forced them back to the ground. With a raised brow, Ben watched the look on the fake king's face as he darted back and forth behind his line of men. The imposter seemed to have no sense of when to give up. He crossed his arms over his chest and glared at Ben's guard. The fake king's sneaky slimy prime minister arrived at his side and whispered in his ear again.

"I have more men..." Mawhorter sneered. "Hidden throughout the castle. There is no way you will succeed."

"Mawhorter..." Ben spoke calmly. "I am sure you have men upon men hidden in so many places I could never think of them. The problem is, I have you. The fight has already been won."

"You don't have me ye..." the man let his voice trail off as a large contingent of Ben's men swarmed up from the back side of the castle and took the new guard in hand. Two rune casters grabbed Mawhorter and the Prime Minister as they attempted to run. Ben pushed through the melee, ducking swords that moved towards him and kicking one man that tried to pull him off his horse. He reached the guards that were holding his prisoners and he gave the imposter an eerie smile. "It's impossible..." the man groused, stomping his foot. "We've been keeping tabs on your populations. You sent thousands of rune casters across the border into our territory. How do you still have so many people to back you?" Mawhorter turned and began to study the men and women ringed around him. "How is it..."

"I like to play the long game..." Ben chuckled as he pushed the fake king and the prime minister into the castle grounds at sword point. "I don't like losing. While I may have been sending all the rune casters to you, I was secretly training them as my Special Forces. I didn't have to call up my guard from my castle because the largest portion of my guard were already here."

"Impossible..." Mawhorter gawped at the men holding his arms while Ben dismounted. "You were my personal guard!" The two men only shrugged their shoulders at him.

"Nothing is ever impossible Mawhorter, improbable maybe, but never impossible. I had my people everywhere. Not only am I not allowing you to enslave more people to line your pockets, I am not going to allow you to steal this kingdom from the true successor."

"I am the true successor!" He exclaimed emphatically with his face turning bright red yet again. "There is no other!"

"Oh, there is definitely another." The guard holding him on the right said with a chuckle as he locked a dampening bracelet on his arm.

"Yes...anyone has to be better than you." The other guard agreed, rolling his eyes and giving the Prime Minister his own personal dampening bracelet. "I think I'd even take the Corrupt King of old to you."

"I've had about enough of this..." Ben growled.

He motioned to the two and they put restraints and gags on the imposter king and the prime minister. He turned his gaze toward the forecourt and waited, holding his breath. There were a few skirmishes behind him as some of the Garian guards thought they could break free from the swarm or tried to press their advantage, but his men held them. His horse skittered nervously from side to side, feeling the nervousness of his rider. He reached down and patted the horses' neck, wondering how long it would take Cael and Juta to secure the castle and find Anna.

He was anxious to see that she was unharmed. He was seconds away from rushing the castle to find her himself when she appeared on the right-hand guard tower. Ben shifted his horse and groaned.

Jorst, the traitor of his own personal guard, had her wrapped in his arms, a dagger to her throat. Even from this distance, Ben could see that she had not one but three dampening bracelets wrapped around her wrists. He knew she was powerful, but there was no way she was strong enough to discharge three bracelets at once.

"What the hell??" Mikal growled as he pulled out of the crowd behind him and faced the building. Astrid pulled her horse to Ben's other side and gasped.

"Looks like we finally found Jorst. I'll even wager that Zura is here somewhere." Ben huffed as he waited for the new demands. All his well laid plans seemed to be crumbling just like the guard wall under his power.

Chapter Twenty

Anna groaned deep in her throat as Jorst pushed the dagger harder into her throat. She could feel the tip of the blade as it sliced the skin. Jorst had been guarding her in the dank dungeon cell for hours until she heard a rumble and grumble and felt the whole earth shake. That was when he had grabbed her and hauled her up to this battlement wall with the knife to her throat. She could see Ben and Mikal in the front of the gathered crowd below her. The whole group was around fifty yards away in the main castle grounds. She was elated to see that Ben's guards were holding the Garian's and not killing. She was even more excited when she noticed that the Prime Minister and the Garian King were being held. She glanced at the bracelets on her arms and bit her lip. She could feel a slight draw of her power. It wasn't a flood and it wasn't complete, but it was enough she could do something to get herself free. She twisted her arms at her waist, hoping they would loosen and fall off.

Anna still knew very little about how the dampening bracelets worked but she had figured out that there was a small stone under the silver. She had smashed both bracelets against the stone walls inside the cell she had been tossed into. The ricochet of the smashing had caused extreme pain in her arms, but she had gritted her teeth and smashed both bracelets several times for good measure. When she checked her progress, both bracelets were now showing the black and white rocks which were now cracked in several spots.

Anna inhaled deeply, digging her fingers into Jorst's arms as he paced back and forth across the wall. Her eyes darted to Ben and she watched as he tracked the man's movements. Neither spoke, waiting for the other to make their demands. Anna rolled her eyes and wondered how long she would have to wait. Ben had less patience then Jorst. He kicked his horse forward, Mikal and Maize behind him. When he was close enough to the battlement walls to see them, he stopped the horse.

"Release her or I will drag you off that tower and give you a personal taste of my power." Ben didn't have to shout since he was close enough to be heard. He only spoke loudly and watched as Jorst paced back and forth on the wall, with her being dragged against him.

"Naw…" Jorst scrunched his face up and waved the knife at Ben. "I'm tired of doing what you say. You have no control over me anymore. I am a direct descendant of the original Corrupt King. I've decided that I am going to rule Garia. You've taken Mawhorter into custody and that leaves the throne completely open. All I have to do is get rid of this woman and it is all mine."

"Rune Points save us! How many people think they deserve to be King?" Astrid called with a grimace. "Does everyone think they are descendants of the true King?"

"Sounds like it…" Ben replied with a grimace of his own. "You kill her and I will pull you from that throne before you can even put the crown on your head."

"You'll have to come and take her if you think you are man enough!"

Anna struggled against the man's powerful arms for a second. She could break his hold with no problem. Mikal and Ben had both had taught her how to get out of this type of hold but she knew she couldn't out run him. That was her true problem. He would just catch her again and she would be right back where she was. Anna pushed with her power and found Ben's white orb and tugged gently. He was more focused on Jorst and his claims of being another direct descendant to the original king. Anna rolled her eyes when Ben didn't respond to her tug.

Pushing her power out one more time, she wrapped a net around Ben's power and yanked hard. She wanted to laugh herself silly when he almost fell out of his saddle. At least he was fully attentive now. His white orb of power flared and nudged her black orb affectionately as he tried to hide his momentary lack of control. Now that he was aware she had control of her power, she focused on the situation. Ben had the Garian guards, Mawhorter and the Prime Minister all locked down outside on the castle grounds. Jorst was currently holding her hostage up on the battlement. She eyed the destroyed battlement in front of them. Ben must have used his rune casting to take that part down. She pushed his orb towards the battlement and he glanced to the side toward the crumbled wall. Ben turned his gaze back to her and narrowed his eyes.

"You see that wall Jorst?" Ben tossed up as he pointed to the stones on the ground. "That is what my destructive powers can do. Do you really want to experience that in flesh and bone?" Ben's gaze moved from Jorst to her and he snarled. "It isn't something I recommend."

Ben didn't want her to use her power to bring this wall down. Well, she wasn't sure what other options she had. She could destroy just the section she was standing on. That should break Jorst's attention long enough that someone could capture him. It would also get her out of his grasp since she would be lying on the ground writhing in pain. She tried to focus on other options. There had to be something she could do that wouldn't hurt her. She could see Ben didn't like the idea she was going for. She didn't like it either.

"My fight isn't with you." Ben shouted this time.

"It is now." Jorst shook his head and cast a sickened glare at the former king.

"We can do this the easy way Jorst. No need to get hurt."

"What would you know?" he sneered. He adjusted his grip on her throat and swiped the rain from his eyes. "You think just because you found the famous black rune caster that you can fix everything. You think just because you are a King that you can best everyone in a fair fight. You are pathetic. You couldn't get one good lick in during a sword fight and you know it."

Anna drowned out the rest of the argument. She focused on the wall and the rain and her power. What could she do to get out of Jorst's clutches that wouldn't end in lots of pain for her? She turned her gaze slightly when she saw movement. At the far end of the battlement, she caught sight of Cael. He was standing there with a knife in one hand and a sword in the other. He was dirty and in desperate need of a change of clothing, but he looked prepared to take Jorst out. Strange that he would turn on the man he had been in cahoots with, but she wouldn't look down on a rescuer at the moment. He advanced slowly toward them.

Anna pivoted her gaze to the other side and let out another breath of relief. Juta was there, holding the door with her short sword in her hand. Now she had rescuers on her level, she had to figure out a way to distract Jorst so she could slip out of his arms. Jorst had returned to pacing slightly back and forth. If she made it colder, the air would freeze and his next step would make him slip. Of course, she couldn't exactly walk on ice either. She was going to have to time this and make it precise. Ice was a better idea than crumbling the wall.

Anna was sure she didn't have the control or the precision to be able to pull it off, but she was going to try it anyways. Focusing intently on the wall under her feet, she thought of the water and how cold it could get. The air began to thicken slightly. Little puff clouds of breath formed in front of her face. Jorst turned, walking the other direction. She focused her power towards the ground he was stepping on, willing the ice to form directly under his feet. She heard Jorst gasp in surprise, his dagger caught the side of her neck as he stumbled, pushing her inadvertently forward. Anna took a step to stop her fall but slipped on the ice. Her arms flew out to try and catch the edge of the wall. The wall shifted and her eyes widened.

Ben must have weakened more of the stone walkway than he had anticipated. Her little ice experiment had broken the wall. While she was only one level above the ground, she was totally unprepared to tumble down to the ground. The air rushed past her, the rain pelted her back, and her face smashed against the cold wet unyielding grass of the forecourt.

Anna vaguely heard shouts from several directions. She heard the distinct sound of metal clanging against metal, and then she let out a loud grunt of pain as her body was flipped over. The rain was slowing, sunshine was beginning to peak through the gray thunderclouds, and Ben's handsome face swam up into her vision. Blinking tears out of her eyes, she smiled but stopped as the sharp pain clouded her vision. A warmth began to spread across her shoulder, her face, and her arms. As the pain slowly began to subside, she caught sight of Maize working to heal her broken body.

Swinging her gaze once more to Ben, she felt relief wash through her when she saw the hint of a tear in his eyes and the reassurance of her safety. She had harbored a slight amount of fear that he had put her in the dungeon, but after seeing his face now, she knew he truly loved her. He would never have put her in the dungeon. This was all the work of the Mawhorter's because they thought she was the lost princess. Anna tried to shake her head and smile but hissed when a flare of pain caught her off guard.

"You are unbelievable woman..." Ben growled. He worked the dampening bracelets off her wrists as he waited for Maize to finish healing whatever had broken during her fall. "Only you would come through all of this trying to put a smile on your face."

"Only because I am thinking that I have been kidnapped...yet again...and yet you still came to rescue me. You might want to find a warrior woman to marry instead. Someone you don't have to waste time on rescuing." Anna hissed when one of her broken bones popped back into place.

"I will rescue you forever if that is what it takes." Ben pressed a light kiss to her forehead. "Besides, if things would calm down, Mikal and I could actually get you trained properly to thwart kidnapping attempts."

"She's good now..." Maize shook her head in astonishment. "She broke her cheek and jaw, both her collarbones, and her left arm. I'm actually surprised she didn't pass out from that alone. Move gently for the next few hours. You are going to be very tender."

Anna yelped as Ben yanked her up off the ground and into his arms. "I'll carry her. We have a long evening ahead of us."

"Whatever you say, your highness." Maize dipped a curtsy and ducked away from the group.

Anna wrapped her arms around his neck and sighed. It felt good to be safe and in his arms. She waited for the moment he would set her on her feet so he could climb into the saddle of his horse and pull her up, but that moment didn't come. Ben kept walking and she cracked open her eyes and glanced around. They were inside the Garian castle. There were guards being held by his men in the halls. If this castle was set up like his, they were heading to the throne room.

She glanced up into Ben's determined face and hissed. What the prime minister said couldn't be true. She couldn't really be some long-lost princess. It was just too odd and coincidental. She was first his lost childhood friend and love and now she was the lost princess. No, he must be coming into the throne room to claim his victory. She pressed her face against his throat and inhaled that deep spicy male scent that was purely him. The smell calmed her frayed nerves more than anything until he set her gently on her feet. Panic began to well inside her as he stepped back from her.

"While I want to carry you off to a bedroom to check for further injuries, this part you have to do first."

"Do what?" Anna lifted her gaze to his and patiently waited for an explanation that made sense. "I thought you were going to claim this kingdom. What do I need to do as a future Queen Consort?"

"Anna..." he sucked in a deep breath and smiled. "Princess Alana Sageowl...this is your kingdom. My forces may have taken it back for you, but you and you alone must walk in there and claim your birthright."

"Ever since I can remember the only thing I have ever wanted was to be wrapped up in your arms and to forget that there was a world out there." Anna crossed her arms and glared at him. "And now you are going to claim that I am some forgotten princess that needs to claim this kingdom so when you marry me, the kingdom becomes yours? Just claim the kingdom under the spoils of war if you want it that bad, Ben."

"No. You don't..." He groaned and closed his eyes. "I don't want..."

"It's actually true..." Teamalah spoke softly as she entered the hallway. Tears streaked her cheeks as she folded Anna up in her arms. "I wanted to tell you everything for years, but your mother and father made me swear to wait for the right time."

"You're my mother..." Anna sniffled and pulled out of her arms. "Don't tell me Ben has you worked into this scheme."

"No, my precious..." Teamalah stroked her cheek and smiled a watery smile. "Your parents were Aylex and Lily Sageowl. They assigned your care and protection to me as the Mawhorter's broke into their chambers to murder them. I smuggled you out and hid with you in the mountains with the dwarves for a year. When I felt it was safe, I brought you home and Jasper and I raised you as our daughter, teaching you everything I knew about how to be a Queen. You are Princess Alana Sageowl, and this is your kingdom."

"But..." Anna darted her gaze from Teamalah and Ben. Juta shouldered between the two and gazed up at her with pride. "Juta...tell them how crazy they sound."

"It's true child. I was there the night Teamalah smuggled you into the mountains. I know that is how you know the Dwarven tongue. I helped teach you what you needed to know." Juta ignored Ben's gasp as she patted Anna on the hand. "You are the child of the dwarven prophecy. You will free our people from Mawhorter's enslavement. To do that, you must claim your birthright."

"I need a moment here..." Anna leaned against the wall and closed her eyes, tipping her head back. Slight pain radiated through her face and shoulders but she ignored it at the moment. "Not only am I a powerful and an almost unheard-of black rune caster, but I am Ben's lost friend and love from his childhood and now

I am also supposed to run a kingdom?" She opened her eyes and snorted as she looked down to Juta. "Oh, and I am supposed to free my dwarven friends and somehow, I am supposed to be able to save Ben's kingdom from the horrible blight he created...seriously guys? I mean, don't you think at some point I would remember something about any of this?"

"That would be extremely difficult." Teamalah shrugged. "Your father was the most powerful violet rune caster in the realm. He wiped your memory of your parents and inserted Jasper and I into the memories."

"If that is true, how do we break it? I am not claiming a kingdom simply because you all tell me it is mine. It was bad enough thinking about being a consort and assisting in running one. I'm not sure I really want to be in charge."

"Alana..." Ben murmured. He liked the sound of that name rolling off his tongue. He would probably always call her Anna, but while he was here in her kingdom, he would use her name. "You may not believe us, but your father was the strongest violet rune caster there was. Unless he were standing here right now, or we have someone who is stronger, there is no way to break his adjustment of your memories."

"Am I as strong as my father was?" she crossed her arms over her chest and glared at them.

"Child..." Juta sucked her teeth and shook her head. "No."

"Wow...he was that strong?"

"No child..." Juta gasped in disbelief. "No, you misunderstand. You are stronger than both of your parents combined. It's just..."

"What Juta is trying to say." Teamalah interrupted. "Healing yourself physically is one thing. Those with blue powers do it often enough that it is as simple as breathing, but healing yourself mentally..."

"It's not worth the risk..." Ben interjected. "At least not right this minute. With another skilled violet power by your side, I feel confident enough that you could probably break his adjustment to your memories with no ill side effects."

"Fine, then let us find..."

"But right now..." Ben broke in, capturing her hands in his. "Please take our word for it. This kingdom is yours and always has been. They are in turmoil right now since we have de-throned Mawhorter and they need a strong person to take it on. If we wait for your memories to come back, someone more evil and probably greedier than Mawhorter will sneak in and steal it." He cupped her shoulders and looked deep into her eyes. "Do you really want these poor haggard people suffer yet again?"

"No, but..."

"No but's love..." Ben pressed a kiss to her forehead and turned her gently to face the door of the hall. "As the true Queen of this kingdom, you have to do what you must. It is the hardest part of being a sovereign. Having to give up what you want for the good of your kingdom is always first and foremost your number one priority."

"Ok, I get that...but..." Anna ducked under his push towards the door. She turned painfully on her heels and looked down at Juta. "As my seamstress and mentor this whole time, do I pass inspection right now to announce myself as their princess or queen or whatever? I mean, I am not one to care, but..."

Teamalah and Juta both belted out laughter as they tugged her down the hall to a private chamber. When she reappeared in the hall her face had been washed and her hair had been tidied. While her clothing was still soiled and ripped in several spots, she did look more assembled. She stood facing the door to the hall where all the self-important people would be waiting for someone to tell them what was happening. Her knees trembled slightly and her head was beginning to ache. Thrusting her head in the air, she straightened her spine, pushed the door open and stepped boldly into the hall. She was going to claim the kingdom of Garia as hers. She was going to help heal the rift between the two kingdoms. She was going to bring justice for her dead parents. She just prayed she was going to do it all with Ben by her side and her new friends at her back.

Chapter Twenty-One

Taking in the sight of the Enderton grand hall had been awe-inspiring. Even three weeks later she could remember how her knees had trembled at the thought of such a large room with so many people inside of it. The Garian room was much smaller in comparison but still quite large. She stood just on the other side of the door, Ben directly behind her. Her eyes swept from one side of the room to the other. There were servants standing at the back of the room, but the benches were filled with noblemen and women. The benches were made of marble and padded with pink velvet. The walls had been draped with pink velvet, and the braziers had been colored pink. She took steps down the middle walk way and glanced at the portraits on the walls. Each was framed with gold and depicted only the Mawhorter's as the ruling family. She noticed each picture showed them dripping in gold and jewels. Swallowing down her anger at their show of fortune, she turned her gaze to the dais as she reached the halfway mark. Her steps faltered and she suddenly came to a stop. Ben had been walking directly behind her and had to brace her hips with his hands as he collided with her. He glanced over her shoulder and growled.

"Goddess dang...can't we catch a break?"

Anna had never heard a better response than that in her life. While she had been taking in the look of this room compared to Ben's, she had missed the fact that there was a woman already sitting on the throne at the end of the hall. This woman was wearing a bright pink Garian style gown. Her long red hair was swept up into a braid that was wrapped around her head. There were stones tucked into the braid and a crown rested just in front of it. In contrast to Princess Elena in Enderton, this woman had barely used any make-up and was flaunting herself naturally in front of the assembled noblemen. Anna found herself swallowing hard as she recognized Zura, her former kidnapper. Zura stood, a scepter of pure gold held in her hands as she narrowed her eyes at the perceived intruders.

For a brief moment, Anna figured it would be easiest just to turn and walk out. Then she thought about all the things Ben, Juta, and Teamalah had told her in the hall and she firmed her resolve. Ben may have taken back her kingdom with force from the greedy Mawhorter's, but she was going to take Zura off that throne herself. All of the noblemen in this room turned their eyes to her and she swallowed once more before she squeezed Ben's hands and moved forward. She may be wearing her workout clothes, look like death warmed over, and was exhausted beyond words, but she wasn't going to allow this woman to take anything else from her.

"Zura..." Anna called loudly when she stopped at the base of the dais. "I believe that is my seat. You have gone from kidnapping to seat stealing. Isn't that a little low even for you?"

"That's Queen Zura." Zura glanced at all the noblemen who had their heads bent together. The sound of barely restrained excitement flooded through the room as whispers bounced from the aisles. "Where is Jorst? I thought he was finally going to take care of you. He promised we could rule together."

"Take care of me?" She took a step up on the dais and watched as Zura trembled and took a step back, her body immediately hitting the throne. "Why, I'm not sure what you mean Zura. Why would you and Jorst need to get rid of someone as plain and common as I?"

"You know why," Zura squealed with narrowed eyes and flared nostrils. "Guards, take this woman to the dungeons. She offends me."

Two men moved from opposite sides of the hall to take her arms. Anna raised her arms and forced her power out. She moved her arms toward Zura and narrowed her eyes. The two guards moved up onto the dais and stood on either side of the throne. She took the final step up and stood on the dais in front of Zura. "I am Princess Alana Sageowl, true heir to *THIS* kingdom. If you do not remove yourself from my throne, I shall have you removed."

"What gives you the right to claim this throne? There is no way you can prove who you are." Zura stomped her delicately pink booted foot and snorted. "After all, the Sageowls are all dead. There is no way you can prove your claim."

"She can..." an unknown man in the middle of the seated noblemen shouted as he stood and pointed to Teamalah. "She was the princess's nursemaid. Speak the truth Teamalah Forsooth. Is this woman our missing princess?"

"Aye, that she is! She has the birthmark to prove it." There were whispered agreements and denials. Teamalah nodded at Alana and watched as she turned back to the woman sitting again on the throne.

"Prove it..." Zura squeaked like a mouse. "Show us this birthmark. Does anyone even know what this birthmark looks like?"

"Very well..." Anna sighed and was getting ready to turn when Ben caught her arm. He moved so he whispered into her ear for only her to hear.

"Probably not a smart move love. That birthmark is in a spot only I am going to see...well, aside from Teamalah and maybe Juta...that is."

"Oh..." Anna blushed as he released her and stepped back. "Um...that explains why I've never seen my own birthmark. Get off my throne Zura."

"Make me." Zura actually stuck out her pink tongue and dropped onto the throne.

"Oh, for the love of the Goddess..." Anna tossed her hands up in frustration and pushed out her power again. The two guards that waited patiently by the throne stepped up and grabbed Zura by the arms. They hoisted her off the throne and carried her wailing and screaming towards a door set in the far-left wall. Once she was out of the room, Anna turned to the assembled noblemen and women with a frown. She would have preferred it if there were some common people in the room other than that handful of servants at the back. Clearing her throat, she addressed the assembly. "I am the lost Princess Alana Sageowl. I have returned to claim my throne. Do any assembled today dispute my claim?"

Silence met her statement at first. Fear gripped her as she waited. Then the whispers grew louder and more furtive. Anna held her breath as she scanned the faces of the gathered people. The original speaker, the unknown man in the middle of the room, raised his hands and began the cheer. "All hail Queen Alana Sageowl!" She held her arms up and pasted a stern look onto her face. Anna glanced out the door of the hall and caught sight of guards with the prime minister. She was sure the fake king was directly behind them. She waved them inside.

"What shall we do with these two?" Mikal beamed at her as he held the prime minister.

"Show them the hospitality of our dungeon please. I'll deal with them a little later." Anna watched as they were hauled to the side of her dais and through the door that Zura had been taken to. Cael stepped inside with Jorst.

"My lady..." Cael bowed and frowned when Jorst yanked out of his arms and started to run. With one well-placed foot, Jorst fell face forward. Cael yanked him up and stood him back in front of Alana. "What shall I do with Jorst here?"

"Ben?" Alana inquired. "I can send him to my dungeon for holding me hostage twice, but he is your personal guard."

"Was..." Ben snarled. "He is in your kingdom and committed an offense here last. Charge him as you see fit."

"If you would be so kind as to show him the hospitality of my dungeon Cael, I'd greatly appreciate it."

"Yes, my lady." Cael bowed once more and then shoved Jorst off to the side.

"Has anyone laid eyes on the Queen imposter or the Princess imposter?" Mikal asked as he returned to the hall. Their eyes turned to Juta and she gave a vicious snarl before answering.

"Gone...run off before the fighting even started. Our snitch is still at large," Juta answered.

"We can deal with that later then. My first and last order of business for today." Anna projected her voice for everyone in the hall to hear. "Send runners, send pages, send all those able to carry this out to my people. We are NOT at war with Enderton. A Sageowl has returned to the throne and all will be worked out for the betterment of my people!"

Anna watched as the noblemen hesitated and then began to flood out of the hall. When the only people in the room were guards, Teamalah, Juta, Ben and her, she collapsed onto the floor, laid back and sighed. She was exhausted and ready for bed. She didn't have another ounce of energy to do anything else. Her face was throbbing painfully and her headache was growing. She felt a warm body ease down next to her. She turned her head and looked deep into Ben's dark brown eyes. He smiled at her as if she were the sun. She inhaled that spicy masculine scent that was his and looked back up at the ceiling of the room.

"Maybe I should have had two orders of business today...this ceiling needs some serious attention. I mean, a pink ceiling? Who would have thought of that?"

"Yeah...it does look a bit pink..." Ben teased, his fingers threading with hers. "You know if you were tired, you have a perfectly good throne you could have collapsed into."

"Not my style Ben," she tossed back. She began laughing and Ben joined her. "Is there anything else I am required to do today or is it possible to get a shower, clean clothes, and a good night's sleep?"

"Well..." Ben winked at her. "Now that you are Queen, I am sure all of that can be arranged. I just want to curl up in bed with you in my arms. I am glad that you are safe now."

"I like the sound of that as well." Her stomach growled and she laughed again, sitting up. "That's the other thing that needs to be dealt with, I guess. I haven't eaten for several days. You know, even those in the darkest part of your dungeon need to eat."

"I'll make sure I look into that, but keep in mind the only people I had in that section were murderers...so I wasn't inclined to care if they ate." Ben caught her arm and tugged her toward the door.

"Cael was in there and he didn't murder anyone."

"No, but I wasn't prepared to be nice to the man who kidnapped you either." Ben pulled her hand up and kissed her fingers as he sighed. "I guess I need to apologize to him. He has been a huge help in all of this."

"No need..." Alana remarked with a sly smile. "After today, I plan to put him on my personal guard."

"Stealing my people already..." Ben tsked with a smile as they stepped into the hall. They were greeted by the servants that had been at the back of the room. A tall woman with emerald green eyes and fire red hair that was escaping her bun dipped a curtsy to them and blushed.

"Your highness...I am Greetta." She glanced at the entourage that was growing behind her. "I will escort you and your guests to a room for the night. Would you like to be in the royal chambers? I warn you we haven't had a chance to strip the personal items yet."

"Anything clean and quiet will be perfect Greetta..." Alana gave her a warm tired smile. "Please have a bath drawn and a light dinner brought to my suite as well."

"Right away your highness." Greetta turned and instructed several of the ladies behind her. Once done, she turned. "Shall you be...uh...sharing chambers, your highness?" Greetta's eyes darted between her and Ben and her cheeks flushed a red to rival her hair.

"We are not married as of yet..." Alana acknowledged. "But I don't plan to wait much longer. King Braun will be sharing my chambers even though that is highly inappropriate. I assume the servants are all versed in how to keep things private."

"Of course, your highness."

"I think I would prefer it if everyone just calls me 'my lady' or Alana or even Anna...this 'your highness' business is a little too stiff and formal. I have never been higher than anyone and don't plan to act like it."

"Maybe..." Ben remarked as Greetta nodded and turned. They followed her down the long hallway and up the staircase. "We should discuss that first. There is a reason we use that title."

"Ugh...fine...we can discuss." Alana walked into the room that Greetta opened, thankful it wasn't decorated in any shade of red or pink. This room was styled with shades of blue and it suited her just fine. There was a bath already drawn and she instantly gravitated towards it.

"I must go see to the surrender of the Garian troops. You enjoy that bath and in no time, I'll be back." Ben stopped and turned at the door. His eyes sought out Alana's as she sighed in pleasure at the warm water. "Do me a favor and don't get kidnapped while I am gone."

"It will take the Goddess herself to pull me from this tub..." Alana moaned as she soaped off the grime of two dungeon cells.

"I'll consider that a challenge when I get back then." Ben waggled his eyebrows and then disappeared. Greetta reappeared a short time later with several outfits and a nightgown. Only then did Alana pull herself from the warmth of her tub and towel off. She grabbed the nightgown and slipped into the deep purple fabric before climbing into the soft peat filled bed. The moment her head hit the pillow she was asleep.

Chapter Twenty-Two

"Wake up, lovely..." Ben murmured softly as Alana stretched and he kissed the scar on her cheek. It was still dark outside the window. She groaned and buried her head against his chest.

"It's too early..."

"It's never too early." He chuckled as he pressed a light kiss to the top of her head. "We have to keep in shape and get you trained on how not to be kidnapped."

"I'm a Queen now..." Alana stifled a yawn and glanced up into his dark brown eyes.

"Yes, you are."

"Then I decree that I don't rise before the sun peeks over the horizon." She enjoyed the rumble of laughter that filled his chest and growled when he pulled out of her arms. "I made a decree...I'm not rising."

"Well, be that as it may, my love, your royal decree doesn't sway me or my kingdom..." He turned back and stole a quick kiss. "Unless I want it to, that is."

"Ben..." Alana whined as she tossed the covers from the bed and glanced through the outfits Greetta had brought up for her. "I still have a million other things I have to do. We have to free Juta's people, we have to cure the blight..."

"All those things will come in due time my love." Ben wrapped his arms around her waist and placed a kiss on her neck as he picked a dress for her to workout in. "We just have to breathe and remember that everything we do is now in service to two kingdoms."

"One kingdom Ben. Our kingdom's need to return to being one, under the ONLY true heir to the original Corrupt King."

"With you by my side, I think I can handle that..." Ben murmured as they walked out of the bedroom, their fingers entwined, looking for a room they could repurpose to work out in. "I think between us, we can handle just about anything."

"Just the two people I wanted to see!" Mikal said with a flourishing bow as he joined them on the stairs. "We have lots of things to discuss. Most importantly..."

"Mikal..." Ben growled low in his throat as they sized up the ballroom.

"Yes brother, my king?"

"It is way too early for such enthusiastic greetings. Wake the rest of the council, we are going to have our morning workout and then we will hold a meeting."

"Of course..." Mikal winked at Alana as she rolled her eyes and began stretching. "I'll make sure that everyone is ready...but where shall we meet?"

"I guess the study..." Alana yawned behind her hand. It is the only room with a map of the kingdoms and enough space for all of us."

"Perfect. I'll have everyone ready within the hour!" Mikal gave another flourishing bow before retreating from the hall.

. . . .

"BEN! ALANA! WHAT a lovely bright vivacious room to find you in," Mikal called with a broad smile. "Are we talking war or blight?"

"As always, your sense of style is called into question," Alana jabbed as she pulled a chair over to the table. "Both happen to be on the table at the moment."

Mikal claimed a chair by the desk and helped settle Astrid's notes and files onto it. Astrid glanced around, found a dressing stool and dragged it over to settle next to him. The Garian royalty's study had been painted and decorated in hideous shades of green. He was one hundred percent sure that the Prime Minister Jesper had decorated this room. He probably even spent all of his time in here as Mikal couldn't see the actual King and Queen doing any real work. The walls were lime colored. The hardwood floors were covered in exorbitantly fluffy ridiculous looking rugs that were mint green. The chairs had all been redone in gilt paint and artichoke green velvet. The wall coverings were that lovely shade of seafoam to match the cabinetry that was all painted in pistachio. He was absolutely certain that if he had to spend more than an hour or two in this room, he would lose the last meal he ate. He shot an unabashed grin over to Alana as he eased back in his chair.

"Your Highnesses!" Astrid murmured softly as she shuffled her parchments around. "Let me gather my intel and I will be with you in a moment."

"Not without me!" Juta shoved into the room and claimed a seated position on the green fluffy rug. Why anyone would choose something fluffy as a rug, Alana would never ever understand.

"Ben, darling..." Alana chuckled as she rubbed the throbbing vein in her forehead. "We need to get a council chamber made somewhere in this castle. I can't stand the colors in this room."

"Might I insert a thought..." Juta said in her native dwarven language. All turned to look at her, waiting patiently. Astrid shuffled some parchments noisily, glanced up apologetically, then crossed her fingers and settled them on top of the stack. "It seems to me since you two are planning to wed and unite both kingdoms that it would make logical sense to either choose one castle over the other...or," Juta paused for maximum effect, watching to make sure everyone was looking at her. "Build another castle to unite both kingdoms under neutral ground."

"So sorry!" Cael apologized as he stepped into the study. He closed the door, leaning against it as everyone continued to stare open mouthed at Juta. "Damn, I always miss the important things. What has the impossibly vertical challenged wise woman revealed now?"

"Is that realistic?" Alana inquired as she finally closed her mouth and tilted her head. "Just build another castle? I mean we already have two at our disposal. Isn't that a little too lavish? All the land in the kingdom has been divided up and parceled out. If we pick another location to build a castle, that would take land from someone, right?"

"It is practical, love..." Ben chuckled and patted her on the head. "All we would have to do is pay the person you are taking the land from. It makes perfect sense and I'm not sure why I didn't think of it already."

"You simply don't have the years of experience I have..." Juta sniffed, turning her head and crossing her arms. "Enough of castles and moving. What are we talking about today? War, blight, memories, the missing pseudo-Garian royalty?"

"We need to discuss all of that eventually. First, I want to apologize to Astrid, Ben, Mikal and Juta for hating you all when we first met. I thought you were killing rune casters and couldn't believe you would commit such a heinous crim. Then some of my memories returned and I knew that it all had to be a lie." Alana gave a soft smile as she focused on Astrid. "I have learned that you Astrid are not as evil as I thought. I am so sorry."

"All water under the bridge, Your Highness," Astrid said with a bright grin.

"Next I want to apologize to you Cael."

"Me?" he gasped. "What for?"

"When you kidnapped me, I just assumed that you were looking to poison me against Ben or going to try and kill me. I now see you only had the best intentions for the people of Enderton at heart."

"No need to apologize, Your Highness." Cael dropped his gaze and blushed. "Thank you."

"Now, let's focus on the two most important topics. Blight and war." Alana looked from one to the other of her council members and waited. "Anyone want to start us off?"

"While I am from Enderton, I have a great rapport with the Garians..." Cael began. "My farm borders one of the blights near the border and so I did a lot of bartering with them. I can tell you for certain, this kingdom is already circling the poor house thanks to King Caurile and Queen Saleeze Mawhorter. If you wage an all-out war against Mawhorter's hidden army, you might lose more than just your armed forces. Food in Enderton is half rotten to begin with. Garia is now sending half their stores to Enderton to supplement but there won't be enough to feed everyone AND an army for an extended war. From the looks of Astrid's reports, we can't win that war in three hours like we did here with no casualties. It would probably be a war of months or years."

"Cael is right," Astrid waved her hands at the reports on the desk in front of her, then looked up and smiled at Cael. "All of my reports are showing that Mawhorter's army is using guerilla tactics on the dwarves, making it almost impossible for us to root them out. They come out only long enough to skirmish with the dwarves and then they run off, crawling back into whatever hole they came from."

Juta sat up slightly taller on the floor and nodded, waving her arms around dramatically as she spoke. "My people are telling me that they have found traces of these foul beasties. They are bold and use the tunnels of my people to hide. For months now my people have tried to root them out like the rotten disease they are but it seems as if they are utilizing some form of rune casting to hide. They are getting bolder, stealing children from the homesteads and bartering them off as slaves with no one the wiser."

"The Mawhorter's did not suffer for rune casters." Mikal flushed red as he glanced over at Ben. They exchanged meaningful looks before he rushed on. "We DID send all of our rune casters here to Garia to train as our hidden army. There was no way to make sure that ALL of them returned to us. I am sure they were able to ferret out several dozen that could hide their tracks well. I'm sure some of them are even aiding the slave traders."

"Why is it legal to own a slave?" Alana demanded as she rested her head back against the chair.

"It isn't." Ben answered. "It hasn't been legal in either of our kingdoms for almost fifty years, but eliminating it is getting difficult for the very reasons Juta has given. When we find someone who has purchased a slave, we punish them and interrogate them. By the time we root out who the slaver is, they have gone into hiding using the hidden market to cover their trail. I sent one of my personal guards that I trusted under guise to root out these criminals, but they came back empty handed."

"Right..." Alana tilted her head. "We must put off saving the dwarves for now because an extended war of tracking and tracing down each and every one of Mawhorter's slavers would cause our people to stave. Are we all in agreeance?" She waited as they mulled over the information and then chorused their agreeance. "Then I guess we turn to the blight. When Bulgar kidnapped me and tried to force me to heal the blight, I forced a good amount of my power into it. I'm not a trained rune caster, but it almost felt as if the blight was a living thing. I felt raw emotion pouring up from the ground."

"Is that even possible?" Astrid inquired as she glanced from Ben to Mikal and back again. "Can you create something living out of rune casting?"

Ben shrugged his shoulders but thought hard about all he had read. "Green runes can make living things grow and blue runes can heal living things. While I haven't seen anything written or heard of anything, it doesn't mean that the rune powers couldn't be used to create a living thing. It also doesn't mean that multiple casters couldn't come together to create something living. The lost books on rune casting might have held a clue but since they are lost..."

"I agree..." Mikal scratched and tugged his right ear. "After all, Astrid is now able to track powers instead of just knowing what type of power a person has. That has never been recorded or spoken of. It very well could be possible that two or three casters working together could create a living essence."

"But we are talking about one person..." Juta snapped her fingers in anger. "One person with white power. Is it even possible for white power of seduction and destruction to create a living creature?"

"Must be." Cael chuckled. He sobered quickly when everyone glared at him. "Well, honestly, think about it. I know I am just an ordinary, but we are debating if it is possible and yet half this land is plagued by the blight. It has to be possible, otherwise we wouldn't be dealing with it. The question is how to eradicate it."

"I think the more important question in this instance," Alana grumbled. "Is how to determine if it truly is a living creature. If it is, should we eradicate it? Seems to me that if it is a living sentient being, we can't just wipe it off the face of the kingdom because it is an inconvenience to us."

"Farmers deal with crop pests and fungi. Would you consider them living?" Cael tossed back.

"Yes and no." Astrid pipped up, crossing her legs and tugging them to her chest to rest her head and arms on. "I think what Queen Sageowl…"

"Alana…" she snipped. "To everyone in this room, I am neither queen, lady, highness, or any other title. You call me Alana or else face the noose." Alana snickered to show she was teasing them.

"I think what Alana," Astrid paused, then started again, this time blushing and dipping her head towards her. "Is trying to say is that if the blight is sentient, which a show of emotions would be proof of, then to kill it is not an option. Pests and fungi, while alive, are not sentient beyond eat, sleep, reproduce."

"Perfect explanation Astrid." Alana tipped her head. "Does anyone know how we can find out if this blight is 'alive' in a sentient sense?" All faces turned to her and shook their heads negatively. "Then we are back at square one. We can't fight the blight without more information and we can't fight the slavers without starving half the kingdom for several years."

"I suggest..." Juta clapped her hands in glee and jumped up onto the desk. She danced a jig and twirled. "We talk about memories and weddings. Those are attainable right now."

"Your Majesty..." Greetta tapped lightly on the door of the study and curtsied. "Beg pardon..."

"Yes Greetta?" Alana was thankful for the interruption as she rose from the chair and headed towards the hallway.

"There is an urgent matter that needs attention."

"Of course..." Alana bowed her apologies to the room as she disappeared down the hall. Ben followed her quickly just to get out of the green room.

"Ungrateful boorish insolent children of elfin leeches..." Juta groused as she hopped off the desk. "I will get my wedding! I vow it! Run for now if you want, but I will not be delayed!"

Epilogue

Ben rolled over in bed and groaned when he opened his eyes and saw the sun peeking through the window. He wrapped his arms around Alana's waist and smiled as she snuggled closer. It had been a little over a month since Alana had ascended to the Garian throne. Since then, he had enjoyed every moment he could spare with her. Mikal, Astrid, and Cael had made sure to work through all of the Garian troops. They had pulled all of the ones that seemed honest and faithful to their cause and released those who more than likely still harbored Mawhorter tendencies. Juta had been working through all the remaining staff and holding interviews to fill immediate gaps. Alana stretched, her body rubbing delightfully against him, causing him to sigh in contentment. In all of his wildest dreams he could never have imagined the pure happiness one could find by just being near the one you loved. He heard her gasp and then she sat straight up in bed, her eyes finding his and her mouth twisting up in a smile.

"Why do I get the feeling I am not going to like what you are about to say?" Ben demanded as he watched the excitement growing in her.

"You are going to love it! You know you will." Alana dropped down and gave him a kiss before throwing the covers off and rummaging through the wardrobe. "Get up lazy bones, we have a lot of work to do!"

"Work...and I'm going to love it?" Ben chuckled but climbed out of the bed and pulled on his breeches. "I think you have me confused for someone else. I never love work."

"Ah, yes, but I promise you'll love this." There was a soft tap on the door and Alana called for them to enter. Greetta poked her head inside and gave her a sleepy gaze. "Greetta! Perfect. Get the council together in the dining hall. We have lots to discuss."

"Yes, my lady." Greetta pulled her sleepy head back out of the room and then opened the door once more. "Do you want cook to make something to eat while you discuss?"

"Uh..." Alana wrinkled her nose. The cook was used to cooking for the Mawhorter's who enjoyed very greasy and heavy foods. "Yes, but something light...and not greasy."

"Yes, my lady..."

"Now..." Alana turned sparkling brown eyes toward her love and smiled. "Let me tell you exactly what I have in mind."

• • • •

"TELL US..." MIKAL YAWNED once more as he watched Greetta and one other woman bring platters of food into the dining hall. He shook his head, knowing full well that Alana would have asked for a light breakfast, and then turned his gaze to his brother. "Why are we all up and having a council meeting before we normally get up and start training?"

"Alana..." Ben sighed as he leaned his head on his hand in resignation.

"I just had the most wonderful idea!" Alana squealed in delight. She looked at each of them in turn and clapped her hands. "Let us host a festival."

"You woke us all up for that?" he groused. Astrid kicked him beneath the table and he grunted. "That couldn't have waited until a decent hour of the day at least?"

"No. I need everyone to help with this." She focused on Astrid and smiled. "I need to notify everyone in both kingdoms as quickly as possible. We need to get supplies together. We need our guards prepped. I had hoped that you could use your birds to get messages to every town on both sides of the border?"

"Yes, but there are a few that I haven't had a chance to train my birds for..." Astrid said, as she eyed the platters of greasy food.

"Our guards are always prepped..." Cael interjected with a yawn of his own. "What more prepping do they need?"

"Our plan..." Ben remarked. "Is to host a festival open to all rune casters and all crafters. We want this festival to draw the most knowledgeable and powerful casters into one place..."

"That is brilliant!" Astrid hollered. She covered her mouth for a moment when she realized that she had talked over the king. Her eyes softened and her normally straight back slumped. "That isn't going to work though."

"We know..." Alana replied. "We thought about those who are still hesitant in thinking that Ben will kill them for being casters, but think of all those that will still come. It will give us the perfect chance to find someone who might be able to solve the blight questions. It could bring us hundreds of casters we never knew of, that could swing the war. It could also find us a violet caster who can help me retrieve my memories. We are working on such limited knowledge when it comes to rune casting. If we can get enough casters into one place working together and sharing knowledge, we might just come up with new information."

"Excellent..." Juta exclaimed with unbridled delight. She had for once been sitting quietly and waiting on the news. Now she crossed her arms and narrowed her eyes at Alana. "I only see one problem."

"There are no problems..." Ben started. He closed his mouth when Juta shot him one of her looks.

"The kingdoms have suffered long enough by being divided. This kingdom fighting with that kingdom. In order to heal the people and quickly, we need to unite them under a common leader. You two must get married. We can't wait any longer."

"What if..." Astrid tossed out. "We have the wedding ceremony to open the festival."

"Exactly my thoughts." Alana nodded and turned to Juta. "I had hoped for an autumn wedding myself, but a spring or summer wedding will also work. It will allow as many of the people from both kingdoms to attend."

"That's all perfect." Cael thrummed his fingers against the table. "Where are you planning to host this festival? Here in Garia where the castle is so tiny a handful of servants can handle it? Or do you plan to head over to Enderton where the castle is so huge that people will have plenty of places to get lost?"

"That is where you all are going to come into play." Ben cleared his throat and took a drink before glancing at them. "We have both decided on the perfect location for a new castle. We are going to build just outside of Honeyvale, smack dab in the middle of the border. Honeyvale and Easton are big enough towns that they can certainly handle the traffic and profit from the extra business. The site for the new castle will be half in Enderton and half in Garia, making it easy access to us for any of the citizens."

"There are no castles in Honeyvale...no building big enough to become your base of operations..." Mikal sputtered. "This is a security nightmare. Where are you two planning to hide yourselves during this event?"

"That is on you three..." Ben replied as he wrapped his arm around Alana's waist.

"Regardless of how dangerous or ridiculous this seems..." Alana picked up. "This will happen. Ben and I both agree it is our best chance of curing the blight. I need you, Astrid, and Cael to work out the logistics of security."

"And what am I to do?" Juta demanded haughtily. She put her hands on her waist and glared up at them.

"When are you all going to stop harassing the wee sagacious lady?" Cael teased as he grabbed a sausage off her trencher and waved it jokingly at the King and Queen. Juta swatted him on the arm, eliciting a lovely yelp.

"You are going to have your hands full planning the wedding and I promise I will stop dodging you." Alana laughed heartily. "Greetta, if you and two of the other ladies could assist Juta with the wedding plans. Ben and I are leaving directly after we break our fast this morn. We plan to travel to Enderton so that Ben can update the day-to-day proceedings that he has put off this month. We will need to start working on combining the staff from both castles. After a week or so we shall travel back to Honeyvale. We can hunt for a place to hole up during this time, rectify any security plans we need to, and get the messages out to begin the festival."

"I'm sure Mikal and I can get the spy network moving for something other than spying..." Astrid winked. "I'd much rather be doing all this, than planning a wedding for the whole entire kingdom." Astrid glanced over and watched as it slowly dawned on Juta that it wasn't just a small wedding any more. Her hands flew into the air, she grasped Greetta by the arm, and yanked her off the bench as they moved to the door.

"COME GREETTA!" Juta hollered. "WE HAVE WORK!"

"Thanks for reminding her Astrid." Alana darted her gaze between Mikal and back to Astrid. "We have complete faith in all of you to handle everything. We will reassess the bigger problems after we get through the wedding and the festival and get the new castle started. Ben and I have several people we are going to stop and see between here and Enderton to get the new castle moving in the right direction. Summons have been sent out already and we should catch them all along our route towards Enderton Castle."

"I wish you swift feet, fair weather, and happy hunting on your path!" Astrid replied, grasping Alana's forearm in an ancient elven parting. She watched as Alana's face lit up and she gave back a common reply as she nodded.

"Always, my sister..." Alana replied, tugging Astrid in for a hug. "Technically Ben is leaving everything under Mikal's hand, but I trust that you will help him with his decisions. Thank you, Astrid, for everything."

"It has been a pleasure Alana..." Astrid gave her a squeeze and pulled back. She watched as Ben wrapped her up in his arms and moved to leave. "You two are just what both kingdom's need."

References

Rune Caster Power Chart

Color	_Physical Trait_	_Mental/Passive Trait_
White	Passion	Destruction
Red	Fire	Anger
Orange	Animals	Endurance
Yellow	Air	Renewal/Power Seeker
Green	Earth	Growth
Blue	Water	Healing
Violet	Spirit	Memory/Foresight
Black	Everything	Suggestion

Acknowledgments

Writing this book has been a dream and a nightmare for me. I have always wanted to become an author by the age of twelve. Well, I missed that mark by about twenty-eight years. Even though it took me forever, this work would not have been completed without the ever-pressing encouragement of my brothers Edmund Mendenhall (may he rest in peace) and Paul D. Mendenhall. I know I am the most frustrating person to live with when I run hot and cold about my writing, but without your continued dedication to helping me research, providing light comedy, bouncing ideas back and forth, and even just telling me to shut up and do it, I wouldn't have been able to complete this novel. It would have ended up in the trash like the five hundred others. I know I don't say it enough but thank you!

I would like to acknowledge and thank all the others who have helped me get this novel out to the world. My beta readers have made all the difference by telling me that my writing was really good (I still don't believe you, but who am I to judge?). The hours you have dedicated to reading this novel, suggesting where things needed to be changed, and just making sure I knew you loved it, helped me get through my insecurities to finally put it out there for the world to see. Thank you from the bottom of my heart and soul to: Paul D. Mendenhall, Carol Anderson, Sandy Robson, Barbara Loyd, Dr. Yen To, and Sheila Harding.

I would like to take a moment to acknowledge the extra special attention that two of my team have put into helping me with this piece. Thank you, Paul D. Mendenhall, for taking on the role of social media expert and publicist. You know I could never figure out the technical side or sell myself to get this novel finished or purchased. Barbara Loyd was a Goddess send as she helped elevate my writing. I thought I was fluent with the English language, but turns out my fingers type faster than my brain can keep up. Thank you, Barbara, once again for catching all my errors.

Lastly, to you, my readers. All errors in this book are mine. I apologize for any glaring plot holes, any major grammar mistakes, and for anything that offends. I hope that you enjoy the book as much as I enjoyed writing it. Thank you for being a logophile or a bibliophile and making my dream a reality.

Don't miss out!

Visit the website below and you can sign up to receive emails whenever Brandi A. Mendenhall publishes a new book. There's no charge and no obligation.

https://books2read.com/r/B-A-RFEU-PKMZB

BOOKS 2 READ

Connecting independent readers to independent writers.

About the Author

Brandi lives in a small town in Kansas with her brother and their senior shih tzu. When not at work, she spends her time reading, writing, quilting, crocheting, and working on her property. She leads a simple quiet life with her family and her dog.

www.ingramcontent.com/pod-product-compliance
Lightning Source LLC
Chambersburg PA
CBHW032045240626
47154CB00003B/1085